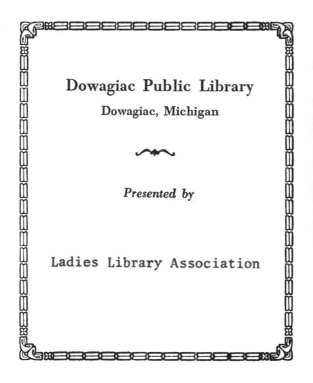

Also by Sandy Landsman

The Gadget Factor

❧ Castaways on Chimp Island ❧

Castaways on Chimp Island

by
Sandy Landsman

Atheneum   1986   New York

Library of Congress Cataloging-in-Publication Data

Landsman, Sandy.
Castaways on chimp island.

SUMMARY: Four laboratory chimps, participants
in an experiment to learn sign language, are placed
on a jungle island to return to nature.
[1. Chimpanzees—Fiction.   2. Laboratory animals—
Fiction.   3. Survival—Fiction]   I. Title.
PZ7.L23175Cas   1986   [Fic]   85-20071
ISBN 0-689-31214-8

Copyright © 1986 by Samuel N. B. Landsman
All rights reserved
Published simultaneously in Canada by
Collier Macmillan Canada, Inc.
Composition by Maryland Linotype, Baltimore, Maryland
Printed and bound
by Fairfield Graphics, Fairfield, Pennsylvania
Designed by Annie Alleman
First Edition

For Wendie

ACKNOWLEDGEMENT

I would like to thank Maurice K. Temerlin, Ph.D., and Jane W. Temerlin, MSW, the real-life "foster parents" of the chimp Lucy, for taking the time to answer a number of questions for me when I was researching this book. Their first-hand knowledge provided some authentic touches and saved me from several errors; any remaining errors are, of course, my own.

Sandy Landsman

Far away in Africa, on Baboon Island, a scientist named Janis Carter is working long and hard at teaching laboratory chimps to return to the wild.

This book is *not* about the chimps on Baboon Island. It is about another group of chimps and their adventures with a very different group of scientists. . . .

Contents

❧ Castaways on Chimp Island ❧

❧ 1 ❧
Kidnapped!

"Danny! Danny!"

I hunched behind the couch.

"Danny! Come out now!"

I knew the voice. It was Dr. Franklin. But I pretended not to hear.

"Danny! Come out or it's trouble!"

Trouble. It was Dr. Franklin's favorite word. Trouble for you, not me! I signed to myself. Trouble for *you*!

"Danny!"

He passed by me. I dashed out from behind the

couch and into my room, crashing a little table over behind me. I slammed the door.

"I saw that!"

I dove under my bed, just as I heard the door open.

Dr. Franklin's voice took on a more menacing tone. "Out . . . now!"

Very quietly, I blew him a raspberry.

Then I heard a little bell ring, and I perked up. The bell meant that Peggy was calling me, too. I teased her, pulling just a little bit at the bedspread so she'd see—and then Peggy's face was grinning at me from the floor in front of the bed.

"Out," she signed.

I let her pull me out.

"You tickle Danny!" I signed. She tickled me; I squirmed and panted.

Dr. Franklin was there now, giving me his stern look.

"Franklin, *you* tickle Danny!" I signed.

He touched his thumb to his first two fingers: that meant *no*.

"You tickle Danny, you nut!"

He sighed and gave me a brief tickle, then frowned again. "School . . . NOW!" he signed.

I got up slowly and gave a hand each to Peggy and Dr. Franklin, and we headed out of the apartment.

"It's the same every morning," Dr. Franklin said to no one in particular. "Every day."

And it was—the same game, same tickles, same

language lab—the same thing. Almost. Except that this was the morning that, in his own way, Dr. Franklin finally went just a little bit too far. Which is really what started the whole story.

But first, you should know who I am. My name is Danny. You've probably heard of me. You might even have seen me on the *Six O'Clock News* or *Sixty Minutes* once or twice before my media career was cut short. But just in case you've been living in a cave for the past four years, I'm a linguistic chimp. That means I'm one of perhaps a dozen chimpanzees throughout the world who have been taught to communicate through something called American Sign Language. Instead of talking as you do, we have a whole language of signs we make with our hands, just as deaf people do. Each sign is a word. In other words, by using my hands I can actually "talk" to people and understand what they "say" back to me. I can also understand some spoken English, but not quite as well as signing.

The language lab was a small classroom in a building across campus. This morning, we were playing a game we'd played many times before. Brian put a picture inside a box and left the room. Then Peggy came in and asked me what I saw. I'd look inside the box, and if I saw a picture of a baby, I'd make the sign by hugging myself; or if I saw a picture of a Mars bar, I'd put the tip of my left thumb to my mouth. It always seemed to me that Peggy could just as easily look inside the box herself; but if that's what they wanted me to do I was willing. And besides, they always gave me raisins when the game was finished. Meanwhile, Dr. Franklin just sat in back and told Brian and Peggy how long to keep going.

Language lab could be fun, for a while. But Dr. Franklin never knew when to stop. He kept me locked in there for hours, after it was just no fun anymore, even if the sun was shining bright and I wanted to be out playing in the park or maybe at home watching TV.

Learning the words wasn't so bad—but satisfying *him* was something else again. It wasn't enough for me to *know* the word. *He* had to have "statistical, scientific proof," which is a fancy way of saying that I had to use the word over and over and over again, just so they could get out their calculators and figure out how often I got it right. So the more words I learned, the longer they kept me in that classroom.

Well, this morning, I don't know what got into me, but for some dumb reason I had to show how smart I was and learn *four* new words. Once I'd gone and done that, I thought they'd *never* let me out. Peggy was nice about it, but Brian (who'd hardly done anything) was so proud I thought I'd be sick. Dr. Franklin kept beaming and popping in with new grad students and professors so he could show me off and then kept testing me again, just to be sure. By the time I got home, not only had I missed *Jungle Man* and *Magilla Gorilla* entirely, but it was already half past *Gilligan's Island*!

Well, that did it. When I got home, I slammed the door and stayed in my room all night and didn't come out even for Peggy.

I was in the lab again next morning, of course—I didn't have any choice. But this day I wasn't playing. I refused to answer any of their questions and didn't make a single sign. I think Dr. Franklin must have realized that he'd gone too far the day before, because he finally let me out after only a little while. Peggy took me to the park, and I got to run around and climb trees and play catch, and I even made it back in time for all my TV shows. All in all I felt great.

I thought about it all that night, and I made a discovery: the less I learned, the less time I'd have to spend in the language lab. I decided to test out my theory the next day, when I "forgot" my four newest signs and absolutely refused to relearn them. This time Dr. Franklin wasn't so easy on me. He kept at me nearly all morning but finally settled for a review of the signs I knew best, and the rest of the session was a breeze. That was when I made my second discovery: it was fun to fool Dr. Franklin.

From that day on, I never learned another word. Oh, I *learned* them, all right—but I didn't let *him* know. And instead of learning a little bit each day, now every morning I seemed to forget just a little

7

more of what I'd learned before. Soon I was down to less than half my real vocabulary. Then I tried a new trick: I pretended to be confused about how to put the words I still remembered together in a sentence. That *really* got him.

I have to admit, Dr. Franklin and Brian didn't just take it, and for a long time they didn't believe it either. They tried everything. They gave me raisins, they gave me more hugs and tickles, they yelled and tried to scare me, they even slipped "forgotten" signs into my favorite games and tried to catch me off guard. But I can be pretty stubborn, and by the time the weather got cool again, they seemed to give up. One day Dr. Franklin looked kind of sad and quiet, and I heard him say to Brian that he thought he had made a mistake, though I wasn't sure exactly what he meant. At any rate, he seemed to lose interest and spent a lot less time drilling me and pestering me and a lot more time typing up his reports back in the apartment. I always got out of language lab right on time now and never had to miss another TV show, so you could say that my plan was a success. I kind of missed how proud he used to be about me, even if he did overdo it, but I'd put a lot of work into this game, and I still remembered what language lab *used* to be like. And, to tell the truth, I still got a thrill out of putting one over on Dr. Franklin.

The only one I didn't like fooling was Peggy. Peggy had a way with signing: the way she moved her hands was beautiful, and her face would just light up when she was saying something. Of all the people who worked with me, she was the only one who really seemed to care about me. Peggy was deaf, so signing was the way she always spoke to everyone. I think maybe that had something to do with the fact that she was the only one who treated me like a person, instead of just an experiment.

So fooling her wasn't much fun. Every evening after dinner, I'd go hide in my favorite corner behind the bookcase and she'd come looking and pretend not to know where I was. Then she'd find me and tickle me on the floor, and after that she'd slip me into my blue Columbia sweatshirt and take me for a walk along Broadway. There were always exciting things to see on Broadway: cars, bicycles, people on roller skates, and all kinds of stores. I'd hold Peggy's hand and look in all the store windows and smell all the foods, and sometimes she'd buy me an ice cream cone or some French fries or a thick shake. And sometimes she'd ask me something, and if it was too hard I had to stop myself from answering and pretend to look puzzled, and she'd just sign, "Poor Danny," and I felt kind of funny.

But I didn't plan to keep playing dumb forever. After all, there was my career to think about. I had a plan. I figured I'd just wait until a TV news crew came in again to film me, and then I'd surprise everyone by getting up in front of the camera and doing tricks and telling them all about myself—using words they thought I had never even *seen* yet—and everyone would finally realize how handsome and intelligent I am. I mean, I've got what's called personality. Some people have it, some people don't, and I happen to have it. When he saw my performance, even Dr. Franklin would have to admit that he'd underestimated me and it was silly to keep drilling me the way he had been. And then the TV station would show the film and people would call in, and I'd be such a hit they'd *have* to give me my own series, where I could do funny things like spilling all the silverware out of the drawer or knocking all the plates out of the cabinet. And Peggy would see me on TV, and I'd sign something special just to her, and then it would be all right that I'd fooled her.

Well, that was the plan. The only problem was, it had been *forever* since I'd begun playing dumb, and still no film crew had come by. I used to be filmed pretty often, but for some reason now it seemed to be taking a lot longer. Finally I began to wonder if maybe I shouldn't have a little talk with Dr. Franklin after all and try to get my career moving again.

But the next day Dr. Franklin was very busy with a lot of meetings and conversations behind closed doors, which I couldn't make out, and I didn't get the chance. As a matter of fact, they were all so busy with meetings and things that they forgot to take me to language lab—for the first time I can remember—so I had a day off.

That evening Peggy came in to see me. Her eyes were red, as if she'd been crying, and I wished I knew how to make her feel better. We didn't go out for our walk that night; instead we just sat on the couch together, and I even let her hold my head in her lap for a little while, which I hadn't done since I was a baby. That seemed to help.

Next morning, Dr. Franklin came into my room and started going through our routine—Good morning, How are you? Are you hungry? The usual nonsense. But this time a few grad students were milling around the door, and so was a tall, skinny man—a guy with glasses and not much hair on his head—who had visited in the lab once in a while. It was unusual to be observed this early in the morning, but Dr. Franklin just kept up the regular routine, and I didn't think much about it.

"Where is your head?" signed Dr. Franklin. It was the first question of our early morning vocabulary review, one of the few exercises I still let myself get right. I pointed to my head.

"Good! Where is your nose?"

I pointed.

"Very good! Good Danny!"

We went through a few more body parts. I yawned.

"Now, Danny—where is your arm?"

11

I pointed to my arm.

"Really? Are you sure? Is that an arm? Let me see!"

I considered signing, "Stupid Franklin!" but thought better of it. I let him see my arm.

"Oh, yes, you're right, Danny!" His fingers circled around my elbow. "This *is* your arm! It's a very strong, good arm!" Dr. Franklin was acting even dumber than usual. "Yes, it's a wonderful arm." The grad students moved closer. "Such a good, strong arm. Can Fred and Brian see your arm also? To see how strong you are? We'll let Fred and Brian see your arm also." Fred took hold of my wrist and Brian laid his hand on my shoulder. Their grips were tighter than I'd expected. Something was not right. I started to move back.

"It's all right, Danny. Silly Danny!" Dr. Franklin signed with one hand, to the side away from Fred and Brian.

Suddenly, I felt a little prick in my arm and saw Dr. Franklin pulling away a needle, like the one the doctor had used at my checkup. I'd been tricked! They'd never have been able to hold me if they hadn't tricked me—not even five of them could hold me! I thrashed about in a circle, knocking over a chair and a lamp, screeching with rage and surprise. Everyone stood very still and watched me.

Suddenly I felt myself losing energy. I circled slowly, suddenly so tired I could hardly stand up. Dr. Franklin came closer.

"It's all right, Danny, just relax. It's all right."

He put his hand on my shoulder and nudged me into the hallway. Then he lifted me—and I was being pushed down into a wooden box! I screamed and kicked, but there was no strength in my body. A few more hands grabbed on to me, then I was in the box, and the cover was shut tight.

They quickly carried me out of the apartment and into the elevator, then outside and into a car. I moaned softly.

Fred looked in at me through the air holes. "Just take it easy," he signed. "It's all right."

But it wasn't all right. I hit my palm against the sides of the box a few times, but the effort was too great. I struggled to keep my eyes open.

Then the car started.

❦ 2 ❦
This is Chimp Island

I woke up with a dull ache in my head. The floor underneath me was rumbling so hard it made my teeth chatter. And the noise: something like the sound of the lawn mowers on campus, but this sounded like *fifty* of them. This didn't seem like any car *I'd* ever been in. And my stomach—I don't even want to *think* about what my stomach felt like —it felt like it had been left behind somewhere, miles and miles away over one of the up-and-down lunges. Underneath it all was a scent making me even more uneasy—something I couldn't quite place. I wanted to be sick—but I couldn't even do that because I hadn't had any breakfast.

When they opened my box, I was too dazed to even think of running away.

"How are you?" Brian signed.

I blinked at him. There was no word I knew that described my condition.

Brian picked me up and carried me out the door of the little room we'd been traveling in. I was hit all at once with blinding sunlight and a baking heat. I covered my eyes. Brian set me down on the ground and tugged at my hand, but I just stood there, letting my eyes get used to the light. I couldn't believe what I saw.

We weren't anywhere near Columbia, that much was certain. The place looked a little bit like the park, but not very much. Trees, shrubs, plants—and as far as I could see, not a building, not a bench, not even a candy wrapper. I was standing on a stretch of sand, a little way before where the trees began; and all around the land was water. We were on an island, just like Gilligan on the TV show.

"Come," signed Brian.

I turned to look at the machine that had brought us here. I recognized it from television: an airplane. I had just had my first plane ride. I wondered why anyone would ever go on one voluntarily.

"Come on!" Brian gave another tug at my hand. I

15

let him lead me into the trees; the shade was cool, and it felt better on my eyes. Just inside the trees was a small clearing.

"Sit," signed Brian, letting go of my hand.

I sat.

In a moment, I heard footsteps behind me. I turned. Walking toward me was the tall, skinny man who had visited the apartment the day before, and on each side of him walked a short, hairy figure that he led by the hand. Could it be? Now I knew what I had smelled on the airplane: other chimps! Just what was going on here, anyway? In a moment, there followed a strange man I'd never seen before, also leading a chimp by the hand.

I blinked at the three other chimps; they looked at me and at each other. I shrank back.

Only one, a boy-chimp, was bigger than I was, but all of them were strangers. The smallest was a girl-chimp, hardly more than a kid. The last one was another boy-chimp, also very young; he looked vaguely familiar, though I felt sure I couldn't have seen him before.

I could feel a pounding in my chest; I wanted to go a million ways at once. My first impulse was to bare my teeth and jump up and down to frighten them all away and let them know they'd better watch out; a moment later all I wanted was to run and hide. In the end, I didn't do either; I just sat where I was, too dizzy and confused to do anything else. I guess the other chimps were in about the same condition I was.

The stranger and the tall, skinny guy spoke for a few moments. Then the stranger waved and tramped off toward the airplane, and the huge machine took off. I was glad to see it go.

"Hello!" said the tall guy. He spoke in a high, singsong voice at the same time as he signed the words with his hands. He smiled encouragingly, stooping to see us better. I looked at him.

A safari helmet sat almost on top of his glasses, hiding what I remembered was a balding spot on top of his head. His face was so long that he reminded me of a hard-boiled egg with a mustache. He also wore a safari shirt and safari shorts, with knobby knees sticking out beneath them.

"Hello!" This time he spoke and signed more slowly, with bigger movements, still giving us that same silly smile. He must have thought we were so dumb we didn't understand.

The biggest chimp looked him right in the eyes for a minute, as if he were studying him. Then he signed back, "Hello."

At least I wasn't the only linguistic on the island. I signed it also, and so did the girl-chimp.

"Good! Very good!" signed the man. "My name is Dr. Simeon. This—" He spread his arms to point out all the space around him. "This is Chimp Island.

17

It is all for you, a special place just for chimps. Do you understand?"

We looked at him blankly.

He slowed down and exaggerated his movements even more. "Whose place is this? *Your* place— chimps' place! This—" He spread his arms again. "This is your new home!"

The other chimps and I exchanged glances. *This,* this grubby island, *home?* The girl-chimp was the first move.

"Home? Home? Take me home now, please! I want home, please! Take me home!" She was on her feet, practically on top of Dr. Simeon, squealing for attention as she signed. "Please, I want home, please!"

Dr. Simeon took a step backward. From the expression on his face, I thought at first he was about to run for cover, but then he took a breath and put on his silly smile again, or smiled as well as he could while chewing his lip.

"Sh. . . ! Listen!" he signed.

"Home!" I figured I'd better get my demand in while I could. Then I remembered I got better results when I used full sentences and said *please.* "Please take me home, please!"

The girl-chimp jumped up and down again, making so much of a racket that even I flinched a little. She was signing "home" with one hand and "please" with the other and giving Dr. Simeon a piteous look.

18

"Sh, sh, sh . . . ! Quiet down, please!" He put a finger to his ear. "*Listen!*" He placed his hand gently on top of the girl-chimp's head. "Sh . . . *Sit* and *listen!*"

She sat down.

"Good!" He tried to look happy, I guess, but he just ended up looking sick. "Now, we know that you all used to live in other"—he started to sign *homes*, then caught himself—"used to live in other *places*. But *we* think that you'll all be very happy here. Chimp Island is like the place your parents came from in Africa a long time ago, the kind of place where chimps are always happy. It's always warm here, so you don't have to wear heavy clothing. You don't have to wear any clothes at all!"

But I like my sweatshirt! I thought. *I wish I had it now.*

"Here you can pick fruit right off the tree, any time you want. There are banana trees, coconut trees, orange trees, papaya—" He looked toward Brian, who was standing a way behind us. "Do we have papaya trees?"

"They're being planted," said Brian.

"Soon we will have papaya trees. And plenty of berry bushes and all sorts of things to eat. Doesn't that sound nice? Do you like bananas and berries?"

Fruits were nice, but I didn't think I wanted a steady diet of them.

I signed, "Thick shake."

"Oh. Well, no, we don't have thick shakes, but—"

"French fries."

"Well, no, but—"

"Hamburger. Mars bars. Coca Cola."

"Well, no, but we have lots of nice fruit and plenty of *new* foods like leaves and bark and—"

"*Home*! Take me home right now, right now!"

Dr. Simeon took a breath. "I know it's hard at the beginning, but just give it a chance—"

"Home—now!" I signed and crossed my arms. I glared right into his eyes.

"No," signed Dr. Simeon. "You *are* home."

How dare they? I *knew* where my home was, and my own room. How dare they try to take it away from me?

"And you know the best part?" Dr. Simeon continued. "There will never be anyone to tell you what to do. Brian and I won't be here very long. No one will say, 'Get up,' no one will say, 'Go to bed,' no one will say, 'Eat' or 'Don't eat.' And no one will ever say, 'Go to language lab'—in fact, there will *be* no language lab!"

Had I seen the signs right? I looked at him directly.

"That's right—no more language lab!"

I stared.

Any other time, I'd have been thrilled; I'd have stood there and done back-flips for joy. But today, language lab was just one more part of home they were tearing away from me. Language lab was what

20

they always insisted on—*always*. If there was no more language lab, then there were lots of other things there'd be no more of, not even a chance of. No more Broadway, no more stores to look at, no more bedroom, no more hamburgers, no more thick shakes, no more tickles. No more Peggy . . . Then I was mad again, really mad. I felt like crying. It wasn't Peggy's doing, I knew that. It was Dr. Franklin, dirty, dirty Dr. Franklin! And then I thought, No more Dr. Franklin, either, not even Dr. Franklin. And, mad as I was, I think if he had shown up right then I'd have run to him, I'd have hugged him, I'd have gone through every sign and language game I knew, if he'd only take me back. But he wasn't giving me the chance. He wasn't there, and he wasn't coming. He'd thrown me out without a warning, without a chance to talk or do anything. Not even a chance. I felt my hair standing up, and I pounded the ground in anger, again and again and again.

"Danny . . . Danny! Calm down!" It was Dr. Simeon, looking more than a little alarmed. "Danny . . . Danny. . . . I didn't know language lab meant so much to you," he fumbled. I glared at him, but I stopped pounding.

"Well, good, that's better, that's much better! Isn't that wonderful?"

He gave me a hopeful look. *I* didn't see anything very wonderful. Then the anger seemed to drain out of me, and we looked back at him blankly again.

21

"Good. *Very* good!" Dr. Simeon fidgeted uncomfortably. He started signing more quickly now. It seemed as if he wanted to be finished with us right away. "We know that you're all used to some kind of house, so, just for the first few days, we built a little shed for you. Just follow the path and you'll find it. Tomorrow, Brian and I will start showing you where to find the fruit trees and berries and other foods. But we know that right now you must all be very tired and hungry, so just for today, we brought along some food for you."

He signed to Brian, who lugged forward some styrofoam buckets I hadn't noticed before and started opening them.

Dr. Simeon began edging away from the clearing. "I know you'll all be very happy to see what good *food* we have for you! We'll see you tomorrow!"

I guess their idea was to distract us with food and then get out of there. But that one day, the trick couldn't work. They were leaving—they were actually *leaving* us!—and food was the last thing on our minds.

"Home!" signed the girl-chimp, squealing at the top of her voice. "Take me Daddy! Take me Daddy!"

I jumped up and down for attention, trying to catch Dr. Simeon's eye. "I want home! Home now please hurry!"

Then there was a screeching sound louder than either of us, and the littlest boy-chimp was pulling at Dr. Simeon's pant leg. "*Eeeeeeeeeeeeeee!* Hoo-*hooooo!* Hoo-*hoooooo!*"

The girl-chimp and I gave a start and shrank back from the noise.

"Yes, Tarzan, what is it?" Dr. Simeon signed above the racket.

Tarzan started moving his hands, but he didn't make any sign I'd ever seen. He just held his hands out, palms down, in front of his chest and made little jabbing downward motions with his fingers, all the while screeching and giving Dr. Simeon a piteous look.

Dr. Simeon looked puzzled. "What, Tarzan?"

Tarzan repeated his strange sign, more insistently than before.

"Now calm down, Tarzan. Sign slowly, so I can understand you. No, that's not a sign! You have to use signs or I can't understand you."

Tarzan grabbed on to Dr. Simeon's pant leg again with one hand and kept up the finger movement with the other, now more and more frantically. "Hoo-*hooo!* Hoo-hoo-*hooo!* *Eeeeeeeeeeeee!*" he screamed. I covered my ears.

Tarzan was crazy, just plain crazy. He was crazy and loud, and I didn't want him there. And *still* he screeched.

"Tarzan, control yourself!" Dr. Simeon tried to loosen Tarzan's grip, but the chimp only held on tighter; Dr. Simeon's voice got even higher than

23

usual. "Stop that!" he squeaked. Tarzan grabbed on with both hands and screeched even louder. "Tarzan!" Dr. Simeon bellowed. The sound was so loud he startled all of us—even himself.

Tarzan dropped his hands and jumped back at the sound. For a moment everything was quiet.

I let my breath out, and so did Dr. Simeon. "Okay," he signed. "Tarzan, why don't you think about the signs you've learned, and then you can tell me tomorrow?"

Tarzan grunted and jabbed with his fingers again, this time without much enthusiasm. It seemed to be all he knew. But at least the screeching had stopped.

"Brian?"

I looked in the direction that Dr. Simeon looked. In the midst of the excitement, Brian had climbed into a small boat just off some rocks by the beach. When Dr. Simeon called, Brian started the motor.

"Good!" I think Dr. Simeon was trying to look cheerful and reassuring again, but he didn't succeed. "We'll see you tomorrow!" He walked toward the rocks.

They were leaving us—right that minute! Without them to show us the way, we might *never* get back!

"Take me Daddy! Take me Daddy!" signed the girl-chimp, jumping and squealing.

I ran at Dr. Simeon's heels. "Please you take me

home now, please! Please show me where home take me home now right now!"

I had to stop at the water's edge. Dr. Simeon stepped into the boat and shouted some command at Brian. Then the motor gave a VROOM sound, and the boat sped off.

The girl-chimp got even more frantic, squealing and jumping up and down on the shore. Tarzan slapped his hand to his forehead and stalked back and forth on the beach, looking at no one. Only the biggest chimp had not moved. He sat at the edge of the clearing, watching the rest of us without a sign of feeling.

The motor sound got softer. I couldn't believe what was happening to me. I watched in a state of shock as the boat disappeared across the water.

⚛ 3 ⚛
Roger and the Insect

So I was alone on the island, with only chimps for company. I thought of spending the rest of my life there—and I was scared.

Suddenly I heard a slurping sound right behind me. I turned around, and there was the largest chimp calmly eating an orange from the styrofoam bucket. My first thought was to fight and grab for my share of the food, but I just couldn't eat right then—and I wondered how the other chimp *could*.

He sucked out what was left of the orange, then chewed the peel up into a soggy wad and neatly licked the juice from his fingers. He smacked his lips.

"I think I can see the mainland out there," he signed. "Close enough to see, but still I wouldn't want to try swimming it."

"What?" I wasn't expecting to see so many signs at once from another chimp, all put together so neatly. He signed almost like Dr. Franklin or even Peggy.

He raised one eyebrow, the way Dr. Franklin sometimes did when he was deciding whether or not I'd really learned a new word. It was just for an instant, but still I didn't like the look, especially coming from another chimp. Then his face relaxed—so quickly that I wondered if I'd only imagined the earlier expression.

"Too far to swim!" he signed slowly.

Now he probably thought I was a dummy like Tarzan.

"I understood you the first time!" I signed. "I just wasn't ready."

"Oh." I thought I saw the flicker of a smile on his face. A chimp can make two very different kinds of smile: one when he's nervous or frightened or excited, and one when he's playing or mocking. It was the second one that I thought I saw.

"Well, I *did*!"

"Of course." He stroked his chin.

I turned away. I was standing on a chain of rocks stretching out into the water, where the boat had been anchored, so I could see most of the island at once now for the first time. It wasn't very big—I couldn't even say if it was larger than Central Park. On either side of the rocks were sandy beaches stretching just a short distance; then came bushes and shrubs and a forest of tall trees with broad leaves that covered most of the island. Beyond the forest rose a steep hill, so I couldn't see any further in that direction.

"Rather limited environment," the other chimp observed.

"Shut up! I don't want to talk to you." I wasn't used to other chimps at best, and I didn't like this one's familiar manner. Just the smell of him made me uneasy. He raised his eyebrows innocently and sat on his haunches.

"They can't do this to us!" I signed. Somehow I felt a little better if I was signing something.

"Can't they?"

I scanned the rocks and the small, grubby island and sat down weakly. They could do it to us, all right. And they were doing it.

"I was on TV," I signed at last. "I was going to be a star." I paused. "How can I be a star if they leave me on an island?"

"Mmm." He grunted. "Yes, well, we all had our expectations, didn't we? I was trained at Harvard, myself, for whatever that's worth." He nonchalantly pulled his lower lip down over his chin. "And I don't think any of us ever imagined that this place would be a part of our future." His lip snapped back to its regular position. "But, until we can figure out a way to get out, I think you'll find that the island does have certain charms."

I stared at him, shaking my head in amazement. For a moment, I thought he must have been crazier than Tarzan.

"Don't look at me *that* way." He yawned. "I don't intend to spend the rest of *my* life here, either. But the fact is, we're here, and we just don't know when we might get out."

Somehow, that didn't make me feel any better. "We've got to get out of here," I signed. "We've got to!"

"Agreed. And I'd be delighted to hear any suggestions."

"Bananas." It was all I could think of to say, so I signed it again. "Oh, bananas!"

"Bananas, oh bananas." The girl-chimp edged her way into our line of sight. "What that? That banana. What color banana? Banana yellow. What color apple? Apple red." It was language-lab talk; she was babbling. "What color berry? Berry—"

"We weren't really talking about bananas," signed the biggest chimp.

"I know."

"Or apples."

"I know."

"You were just practicing."

She nodded.

"For what?"

She gave him a puzzled look.

"Never mind." He yawned again.

"Who are you?"

"My name is Roger," he signed. "And who are you?"

"Mr. Nibbles."

Roger and I exchanged glances.

Mr. Nibbles? I sniffed, then sniffed again. The scent was definitely female—no mistake. I grinned.

Mr. Nibbles stared at us, then looked quickly from side to side, as if searching for a way to escape. "Don't!" she signed. "Don't, don't!"

I stopped grinning, and Mr. Nibbles calmed herself.

"Dr. Denton made a mistake," she explained at last. "When he first got me. By the time he found out, he said that changing my name would have only confused me."

Roger flashed a hint of a grin, too, and then controlled it. "We'll just call you Nibbles," he signed. "Okay?"

"Okay."

"—if you don't find that too confusing."

She eyed him distrustfully. "Don't make fun of me."

"I'm not making fun of you." Roger opened his

eyes wide and looked very sincere, but I didn't believe him for a minute. "Roger is sorry."

"Sorry," she echoed.

Roger nodded.

"Sorry. Nibbles sorry, sorry Daddy. Where Daddy?"

She was edging into that language-lab baby talk again. It seemed to happen mostly when she was upset.

"Where Daddy?" she repeated.

Roger watched her. "You mean your Dr. Denton?"

She nodded. "Daddy will come, Daddy come find me, take me home; he'll find out where I am. Daddy will find me."

Roger and I looked at each other.

"You don't think he knows?" I signed.

"Knows?" She stared at me. "Knows? Daddy *couldn't* know!" She swallowed. "He'd *never* let them take me! He *loves* me, he calls me his little girl! And, and last night he gave me a special banana treat, and . . . and. . . ."

"And what?"

"And he tucked me in and hugged me—and said, 'Be a good girl and take care of yourself.' "

Roger nodded slowly. "He knew."

Nibbles screwed up her face and took a deep breath as if she wanted to suck up all the air in the island, then let it out slowly in quiet sobs. I felt a little like doing the same thing myself, but I didn't. I looked away from her.

"Silly," I signed to Roger. "As long as I get back home, I don't care if I never see Dr. Franklin again!"

"Right. You don't let humans run *you*! You even stopped playing their silly games months ago!"

"Right!" I thought a moment and looked at him more carefully. "How do you know? You don't even know who I am."

Roger gave a little half-smile. "Oh, but I think I do. I believe I must be talking with the famous Danny." Somehow it didn't feel like a compliment. "You know, you were in the news a little while ago."

"A long time ago."

"More recently than you think. See, I like to watch the late-night edition, with the little man signing in the corner for deaf people. I like to know what's going on."

Nibbles gave one more sob and then stopped. She sniffled. I turned back to Roger.

"What do you mean, I was in the news?"

"Well, actually it was your Dr. Franklin. It seems he's changed his mind about you. He went back over what you've done and decided that you never learned language after all. All you really learned was to string some signs together to get a reward: if you make this movement, this movement, and this movement, you get a banana, but you really have no idea that you're making words. According to him, you're really just like—well, like a dog."

"A what?"

"A trained dog," he repeated. "You know: fetch, roll over, play dead . . ."

I was so insulted I could hardly breathe: *How could they think that about me?* Then I felt a sinking feeling in my stomach, and I *knew* how they could think it: my dumb act, my brilliant, miserable dumbact! I'd really outsmarted myself this time!

"But—but that's crazy!" I signed. "I know what I'm saying!"

"I'm sure you do." Roger scratched his nose. "But *something* made Dr. Franklin decide that you didn't. He wrote it all up in some very learned articles."

(So *that's* what he was so busy typing! And right in my own house!)

"And then he somehow decided that none of the rest of us had learned language, either, and he convinced a lot of scientists. Once they decided that, no one would give them any more money for their experiments. You know scientists, they won't do anything without money." He shrugged. "It's not the first time it's been done, you know—setting lab chimps loose on an island. But doing it right takes lots of time and money. This time they want to see if they can do a rush job, sort of an experimental, low-cost crash program. So here we are, guinea pigs again." He looked across at Nibbles, who was now watching us. "I think we all have to thank Danny for landing us on this wonderful island."

"Liar! Liar!" I jumped up and down and screeched. "Dirty liar!"

Roger wrinkled up his forehead and looked at me mildly. "Well, I guess you know best."

"I did not land us here!"

Nibbles sat down and sucked her thumb. "I don't care how we got here. I want home!"

"Well, yes," signed Roger. "I think you've cut to the heart of the matter."

I grabbed my chance. "We need a plan!" I signed and looked importantly at Nibbles and Roger. I knew I'd feel a whole lot better about dealing with them if I could at least be in control.

"Yes?" signed Roger.

"A plan to get us back to our homes!" I signed. We pulled ourselves into a huddle.

"Well?"

"Well . . ." This was as far as I had thought. "Well . . ."

Tarzan knuckle-walked up to a short distance from our circle and peered in at us. I didn't like the feeling of having him around, especially while we were planning; but still, he looked so alone, I thought maybe we should at least let him sit down. I wondered what Roger would say. I stopped my signing and looked from our circle to Tarzan and back again.

Roger caught my meaning. "That insect? We don't have to worry about him!"

"I just thought—"

"Forget him."

Nibbles widened her eyes in concern. "Don't talk about him like that! He'll see you!"

"So?"

"You'll hurt his feelings!"

"How? He can't understand! See—look at this!" Roger walked up to Tarzan and stood facing him, making a friendly hoo-sound in his throat. "You're just a big, dumb insect, right?" He signed in the slowest, most exaggerated way possible, grunting and nodding his head up and down. "Insect, right? You're a dumb, stupid insect!"

He kept up that way, giving the friendliest looks and saying the same things over and over. Tarzan just looked at him, trying to follow, and pretty soon Tarzan was nodding his head up and down along with Roger. In another minute, Roger was coaching him to point to himself and make a clumsy sign for insect—and, believe it or not, the looney was actually doing it!

Roger gave us a wink. "See? He says it himself— he's an insect!" Then he burst into laughter. I had to laugh, too; it felt good to know that I was smarter than at least one person on the island. Even Nibbles laughed quietly, wiped her eyes, and kept on laughing.

Well, it didn't take Tarzan long to see that he'd been made a fool of. He scowled and stalked off with his knuckle-walk, giving us a dirty look over his shoulder. He sat looking out over the water, and we could hear a stifled squealing sound coming from him.

Nibbles had stopped laughing. She kept looking back at him with her eyes wide. "Maybe we shouldn't have done that," she signed.

I felt a little strange, but still it had been so funny, and he was such a looney—but still, I did feel a little strange.

Roger pounded the ground a few more times and then controlled his laughter. "Why not? He's just some dumb animal."

Tarzan squealed again—very high and quiet, as if he were struggling to hold the sound in. Nibbles looked at her hands for a long time. She was signing in very small movements, just kind of halfway making the signs—the way I do sometimes when I'm talking to myself—so I couldn't be completely sure of what she was saying, but it looked something like, "Bad Nibbles, bad Nibbles." She was very quiet, and I felt kind of funny again. Then she got up and walked over to Tarzan. As soon as she got close, he wheeled without warning—snarling and screaming, his hair standing up so he looked twice his size. In an instant she was scampering back to us, with the most shocked expression on her face I've ever seen. Tarzan was just glaring quietly at us now, and then Nibbles started sobbing. "He didn't have to do *that!*" she signed.

Well, that settled it. I'd felt a little sorry for the guy before, I admit, but now I could see that we'd been right about him all along. There was no telling *what* he might do.

"As I said," signed Roger, "an animal." He fixed his eyes on me. "And now, I believe Danny was about to tell us all about his wonderful plan."

❦ 4 ❧
My Wonderful Plan

Nibbles controlled her sobs, and Roger gave me a very quiet respectful look, waiting for me to begin.

"Well . . ." I signed. "Well. . . ."

I looked out to the water, beyond where Tarzan was sitting, and grabbed the first thought that came into my head. "Well, they have a boat, right?"

"Right."

"So the next time they come over, we find a way to sneak into their boat and hide there. Then they take the boat across the water, we sneak out again when they're not looking, and we're set."

Nibbles and Roger just looked at me. I could see

a couple of holes in the idea, but maybe the others wouldn't notice.

"Well," signed Roger at last, "that is indeed a wonderful plan."

"Thank you."

"But *how*?" Nibbles broke in. "How do we hide in the boat?"

"Oh." I wasn't ready for this. "Well, maybe if we wait till they're not looking and—"

"Yes, how?" signed Roger. "And more important, why?"

" 'Why?' "

"Yes, why? Where does it get us? Supposing we do find a way to hide in the boat and manage a daring escape—then what? Then we're somewhere on the mainland, hardly any closer to home, and with no idea at all as to how to get there. We might not even have the food growing for us there that we've got on the island. I'd rather stay here."

For a moment I was just shocked. I couldn't even sign. Back home, almost *anything* I signed was wonderful, just because *I* signed it. And as for an original *idea*—if Peggy or Dr. Franklin had seen me sign that, about the boat, they'd have gone bananas! But not Nibbles and Roger. They were picking, finding fault. It wasn't fair.

I caught my breath. "So what's *your* great idea?" I stood up over Roger and glared down at him. "Just stay here till we rot?"

"Not at all." Roger stayed on his haunches, looking up at me; he touched my hand mildly. "But we'll never make it on our own. Even if we did, once we got home they'd only send us back again." He grunted emphatically. "No. I think our only hope is to somehow make the scientists *decide* to take us back. And now, Nibbles, you may well ask how, because that requires some thought."

I stood there feeling foolish for a moment, with nothing to say; then I kicked at a small stone and sat down again.

So Roger was taking over. And I couldn't even argue, because, so far, what he said sounded right. That was the worst part of all.

"Maybe if we ask them very nicely?" signed Nibbles. "I mean, really, *really* nicely this time."

I spat on the ground. "Oh, that's terrific. 'Please, Dr. Simeon, we'll be good, Dr. Simeon, we *love* you, Dr. Simeon!' "

"Well, why not?" Nibbles seemed on the verge of crying again.

"Because it's disgusting, that's why not! I wouldn't be caught dead signing garbage like that! And besides . . ."

"Besides, what?"

"Nothing."

Roger smiled again. "I believe Danny was about to say that we already tried that—or, more precisely, you and Danny already tried that. Of course, that

40

must have been before Danny decided he'd rather be caught dead than sign that kind of garbage."

"Oh, bananas!" The guy was spooky. I mean, it wasn't even safe to *think* around him. "Look, they're not so smart—maybe we can find a way to trick them!"

Nibble's eyes got wide. "You mean, *lie* to them?"

"Why not?"

"But lying is *bad!*"

"Now, Nibbles—" Roger made a clicking sound in his throat. "Danny didn't exactly say *lie* to them. He said *trick* them, make them think what we want them to think. That's not quite the same as lying, now is it?"

Nibbles looked at him blankly.

Roger rubbed his chin. "Well, let's skip that for a moment. Any plan we make to get them to take us back is going to take time. It took time for them to decide to send us here, and it's going to take more time for them to decide to take us back. As I see it, that means we have three things to think about. First of all, we have to develop a long-term plan that will make them change their minds about us. Second, we'll have to find a way to keep Brian and Dr. Simeon here with us as long as possible, to give us a chance to work on them. We'll have to find ways of acting absolutely helpless—make them think we'll never survive if they leave us."

I watched Roger's signs, and all of a sudden, it

was there, the question I'd been trying not to think about all morning. There it was, and I couldn't ignore it.

"*Will* we?" I swallowed. "Will we survive if they leave us?" Just signing it gave me a sickening feeling in the pit of my stomach.

Roger grunted. "We might."

"We *might*?"

"That's the third thing to think about: survival on this island. Learning what to eat, what not to eat, what to watch out for. We'll have to work at it."

Nibbles looked at me, then at Roger. She was thinking the same thing I was. "You mean, stay here?"

"I mean, be able to do it if we have to. I think we should face it: We may be here for some time."

Nibbles and I looked at each other. It was one thing when the scientists told us that. Coming from one of our own, it was even worse.

I glared. "You mean, start living on leaves and bark, like Dr. Simeon said."

"And fruit, of course—lots of fruit." He smiled faintly. "Not to mention termites. I'm told they're quite a delicacy."

My stomach did a series of flip-flops. "*You* eat termites, Roger! *You'd* probably like them!" Roger just looked at me. "I'm not going to live on that stuff! I'm not! I'll die first!"

Roger scratched his chest. "You may get that

choice, Danny." He paused. "But it probably won't come to that." I let the subject drop and tried to forget about it.

"Anyway"— Roger made a smacking sound with his lips— "anyway, we've got the styrofoam bucket, at least for the moment. So let's think about the first thing, our long-term plan. Danny, you suggested a trick—making them think what we want them to think. Okay. Let's put it another way. We want the scientists to *do* something, right? We want them to take us back. In the lab, they want *us* to do things all the time, and so they use a 'reward' to get us to do it. To reward a chimp, you use a banana treat."

I shook my head. "I always got raisins."

"Or raisins, then."

I nodded.

"To reward a rat, you use cheese." No one contradicted him on that one. "To reward a scientist, you use . . ."

I thought of Dr. Franklin. "A cheeseburger?"

"A cup of coffee?" signed Nibbles.

Roger paused for effect, then rubbed his fingers together in a single sign. "Money."

"But we don't *have* any money!"

"No." Roger smiled knowingly. "But we can make them think that there's money in *us*."

Nibbles and I exchanged puzzled glances.

"Have you noticed anything strange about Dr. Simeon?" Roger continued.

"Plenty," I signed. "He's got knobby knees and a funny voice and he trips over his own feet."

"Well, yes. But I was thinking of something else: How about the fact that he signs to us?"

"What's so strange about that?"

"Nothing," signed Roger. "Except that the reason we're here is that they decided we didn't really know language. But if Dr. Simeon is signing to us, then they're not all so sure. Of course, he *could* be signing just for *me*, but I don't think so."

I didn't like that remark. "Why would he sign just for you?"

"Well, I think they think there's a pretty good chance that *I* really did learn language, but that it doesn't really count. They wanted to experiment with just ordinary chimps, and I think they've concluded that I'm something of an exception."

"What do you mean, an exception?"

"Well . . ." He rolled his tongue against the inside of his upper lip, making a casual inspection of his teeth. "The actual word they used was genius."

"Oh, really." If it was possible, I hated Roger now even more than I had a moment before.

"Well, just keep that in mind. We may find a way to make that work *for* us. The main point is, they're not all sure that we *can't* talk; and if enough of them believe we can, then they can get their research money back and they'll return us to our homes."

It took a moment for it to sink in; when it did, I

almost felt like crying. "So . . . all we have to do is start signing to them a lot, and they'll see that they were wrong?"

"It's not that simple."

I let my breath out. *It never is*, I thought.

Roger continued. "If we do only that—just continue our usual signing—they'll still say we're just repeating things by rote. Brian and Dr. Simeon *might* believe us, if they're here to see it for themselves, but the others never will. No, we need something unmistakable, something dramatic. Something even *they* can't miss." For once, Roger seemed to be groping for words. "Something—" He reached outward toward something I couldn't see. *"Something . . . to make them treat us as we deserve."*

Despite myself, I felt a stirring at his words.

"What do you mean?" signed Nibbles.

Roger stood slowly, with importance. "Well, chimps, it all comes down to one simple question: What do we really want? Will we be content to resume our roles as lab animals for their experiments, to be probed and studied at their convenience and then discarded like so many maze-running rats? Is that what we want?"

"No!" I signed.

Roger pounded his chest once, twice. "I can't speak for you other chimps," he continued, "but as for me, if that's all there were to be gained, I'd rather stay here on this island, a free chimp! No, if we come back, it must be on our own terms, as equals! We'll show them who we are. Then, when they want us back, they must let us have what *we* want!"

My mind was racing. I knew that Roger was taking over, and using words to do it, and I hated him for that. But at the same time his words affected me. Despite myself, I had a funny feeling in my chest— an excitement I'd never felt before. A moment earlier, I'd have been happy to go back under any terms; now, all my old dreams came rushing back to me. "You mean, when I go back, *I* can be the boss?"

Roger nodded.

"And I can even be a movie star?"

"If that's what you want."

"And have my own house and car and a color TV?"

"Of course!"

"I just want my daddy," signed Nibbles.

Roger placed a hand on her shoulder. "Then you shall have him!" he signed.

"What about you?" I signed to Roger. "What do *you* want?"

Roger got very quiet. "Not much," he signed in small modest movements. "I'm only a scholar. I don't need to be a media star. I don't need a house or a car or a TV. I don't even need the love of my 'daddy.' All I want is to continue my studies."

46

I was stunned. "You mean—back to the *language lab*?"

"No," Roger signed quietly, "never in the language lab. I will go back as a simple researcher in language studies."

We were quiet for a moment. I tried to imagine what Roger could see in his goal, but it was beyond me.

"But *how*?" signed Nibbles. "How will we do it?"

Roger smiled. "I'm afraid I'm not quite as quick as Danny. I don't have anything you could call a plan yet."

Nibbles's face fell. "No plan."

"But I *do* have some ideas to work out, and a brain to think with, and an island to explore." Roger drew himself up. "Let's take a walk, chimps!"

༉5༉
Cannibals!

"But where are we going?" signed Nibbles.

"Exploring," Roger answered. We filed behind him on the path, munching the fruits and sandwiches we'd picked up from the styrofoam bucket. We'd left Tarzan behind on the beach. "The more we can find out about this island, the better it will be for us. For ideas *and* survival."

I didn't exactly see how exploring the island would help. But just the same, I felt better now that we were on the path. At least now we were *doing* something, moving around, seeing where we were. Nibbles seemed to feel the same way; she kept running ahead to look at every new flower or insect, then hurrying to catch up with us again as we passed her by. She reminded me a little of a puppy I used to see in the park sometimes.

The path got narrower as the trees and bushes grew more thickly. Thorns scratched my ankles.

"For instance—see that spot over there?" Roger turned and pointed to a clearing, where hills on three sides sloped down to a flat area in front of a cave. "That could be a natural staging area."

"A what?"

"Don't worry about it. Just keep it in mind."

The hair on my back bristled. "Don't tell me, 'Don't worry about it.' What do you mean, a natural staging area?"

Roger gave me his mildest look. "Why, only a place to perform. You do want to be a star, don't you?"

I nodded—though I didn't see how that would help us now.

"I don't know, either," signed Roger, reading my mind. "Not yet, at least. We'll just keep it in mind."

The path veered to the right and then climbed along a hill. We'd finished our food, so we stooped to all fours to climb the path better. All at once a breeze started, cooling us a little in the hot afternoon and rustling surprisingly loudly through the leaves above us; the sound was all around us, and for a while it was all we could hear. Then the breeze stopped—as suddenly as it had begun—and I could hear something else, sort of a soft, rushing sound, not far away. The sound got louder as we continued, and in a moment we came to a stream.

Nibbles was behind us again. She came running up and stopped when she saw it. Then she made a sign: water. I bent down and drank, slurping it up with my lips; it was fresh and cool. Then Roger drank, too, even more noisily than I did, and splashed water up all over his face. Nibbles scooted up next to us and watched closely, looking intently from Roger to me and back again—but she didn't drink. I figured maybe she wasn't thirsty.

We got back to the path again and continued climbing. We were only a short distance from the stream; but already the trees were so thick we could hardly see in front of us. The sweat trickled down my body. Then, through a break in the leaves, I thought I caught a glimpse of something. I quickened my pace—and there, around the next bend, I saw a small building made of unpainted wood.

"I believe this must be the housing they so graciously provided for us," signed Roger.

Civilization! Nibbles and I raced ahead to get a look. I circled to the front—and stopped right where I was. I don't know exactly what I had expected to see: probably something like my room at home, with a door and real walls and a bed and a chair and maybe even an electric lamp. Instead, there was nothing but a shed: three walls, open on one side, with a roof. I could see daylight through the spaces between the wooden planks. Four mats took up most of the space on the dirt floor; the whole building was maybe half as large as my room at home.

Nibbles and I looked at the building and at each other. At last I signed. "This is where we're supposed to *sleep*?"

Roger stepped quietly behind us; we turned. "As you can see," he signed, "no expense has been spared."

"But it's *dirty*!" signed Nibbles. "It's not nice." Her lips trembled.

Roger put his hand on her shoulder. "I know it must be very hard for you."

She nodded.

"Very, *very* hard."

I felt a flush of anger.

"It's hard for me, too, you know!" I jumped in front of them, baring my teeth. "I don't like it, either!"

Roger turned only halfway toward me. "I'm sure you don't," he signed—as if he even cared. I wished I could bite him.

I hated it—the house, the island, the whole situation. And Nibbles wasn't helping. Just because she was the youngest, she got all the attention, and Roger got to act like a big shot.

She sneaked a look at me, then quickly looked away. She could tell I was mad. I watched her standing in front of that dirty shed, her face twisted awkwardly to one side, and suddenly, she looked small and scared. For the first time it hit me how much younger than the rest of us she really was. No wonder she needed her daddy. I felt sorry I'd gotten so mad at her.

"Nibbles," I sighed at last. She looked at me. "It will only be for a few days. We'll get out of here."

The expression on her face softened. "You really think so?"

"Yeah," I signed.

"Well, Danny," signed Roger, "we'll be very happy to hear any plans you may have." With that he strode out into the path. I stared angrily after him for a moment and then followed.

The path led further up the island's one big hill. Along the way we passed banana trees, coconut trees, and berry bushes. I'd done some climbing in the park, of course, but the trees were never as big as this. I hesitated a moment, then swung up into a coconut tree, and had to climb almost as far as I'd ever done in my life, just to get to the coconuts. I felt a little giddy getting up that far. I kept glancing down and wondering if this was all really such a good idea. But then, once I was there, it was nice sitting there and looking around and just feeling the breeze, without Peggy or Dr. Franklin frantically signing or calling for me to come down, and I decided that it really wasn't such a bad idea, after all.

I threw down a coconut and climbed down again. Then we banged it against a rock until it broke, and we all ate some of it. It was a lot sweeter than coconuts I'd gotten from the store back home, and the juice was good, too. Not as good as a Coke, of course —but I was glad to have it, just the same. The berries on the bushes were small and sour, though, and not nearly as good as the ones at home; I took a whole mouthful before tasting them, and I nearly gagged. I had to spit them all out, and my mouth was all sour and puckery. I wished I had some more coconut milk to wash the taste away, but I didn't feel like doing all that work again just for a little drink.

I could hear birds all around me now—a lot more than in the park at home. They seemed to be everywhere. We also saw some little animals like squirrels, who froze and then ran away from us, but nothing bigger than that. We were almost at the top of the hill when the path turned again, and suddenly disappeared into a barrier of thick foliage. Incredibly thick, much too thick to walk through. There wasn't even a good climbing tree nearby to use to swing *over* the barrier, so we had to bite and tear at it for a long time to make an opening.

Roger was the first to squeeze through. Nibbles and I had to hurry after him to where the path began again.

"Maybe from here we'll be able to see the other side of the island," Roger was signing. "The hill goes—"

Roger stopped and stared. In a moment Nibbles and I caught up with him and we stared, too. There, in the path ahead of us were footprints, coming up from the other side of the hill up to the foliage barrier and then circling back again. Footprints— but not like any I had ever seen. Roger knelt and examined them, looking first at his own prints and then at the prints ahead of us. I examined them also.

"What is it?" asked Nibbles.

Roger shook his head.

There seemed to be at least three or four sets of prints. Each looked a lot like a chimp print—the bare feet, the long toes—but with one big difference: down the center of each footprint ran a long, thick line, connecting each footprint with the one behind it. They looked something like this:

"Do you think—do you think maybe it was some kind of a monster?" Nibbles signed.

"There's no such thing!" I signed back. But looking at the prints, I wasn't so sure.

"Chimp prints," signed Roger. "Chimp prints that have somehow been changed."

That much was clear. But how, and why? An idea flashed into my head.

"Maybe—maybe it's a tribe of savage, wild chimps that put poles through their feet!"

Roger examined the footprints and nodded. "I think you may be right."

"Maybe they're even cannibals!"

Nibbles shuddered.

"Possibly," signed Roger.

For a moment, I felt glad to have figured it out and been right. Then I felt a chill go down my spine, and I wished Roger had said that it couldn't be.

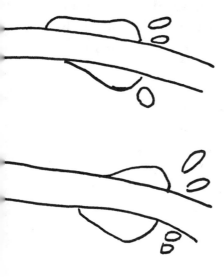

"Do you really think so?" I asked.

"Possibly," he repeated. "At the least we know that we're sharing the island with some other chimps or chimplike creatures." He looked at the footprints again. "I'm going to follow these a little farther and see what I can find. You two stay here."

I didn't argue.

"I'll be back soon," he signed. Then he disappeared around a bend into the foliage.

"Oh, I know it's the cannibals!" signed Nibbles.

The pad of Roger's footsteps faded in the distance.

"Maybe they'll get him!" I signed. I had mixed feelings about the idea.

Nibbles looked at her hands. "Don't say that!"

We waited.

It seemed a long while until Roger came back. Then I heard his footsteps, and he clambered down the path.

"Did you find anything?"

Roger shook his head. "Whatever they are, I think they must be somewhere on the other side of the island. As long as we stay on our own side, we should be pretty safe."

Nibbles let out a sigh.

I looked up at the sky. The sun was already getting low, moving down toward the beach.

"Time to head back, chimps!" Roger started down the trail. "We have to be up early tomorrow, so we can plan for when Dr. Simeon comes back. Come on!"

Nibbles and I followed.

It was already sunset by the time we reached the shed. The sky lit up in oranges and reds and even purples, and a hundred other colors it never showed in the city. Nibbles and I stood there looking out at it, and for a moment I was glad we were there to see it.

We went down to the stream again, and Roger and I drank—we really needed it. But Nibbles still just watched, her face almost on top of mine, licking her lips, but still not drinking—and I realized she'd had nothing but a few mouthfuls of coconut milk all afternoon.

"Water," she signed. She wasn't asking us for it—she was just identifying what was in front of her.

All at once I understood. "Dirty. Don't drink dirty." Peggy had signed that to me a hundred times. It was one of the first things I'd learned on our afternoon and evening walks. Don't drink from puddles, don't drink from birdbaths, don't drink from the lake at Central Park. Dr. Denton must have told Nibbles the same thing. And she still believed him.

"Water," she signed again and pressed her face closer to watch me drink.

She looked at the water, then at me, then at the water again. Then she took a breath and bent down to the water; she drank. When she got up, her face had a strange expression, somewhere between fear and relief—as if she couldn't quite believe that nothing had happened to her. She added another sign.

"Good," she signed with a bewildered look. "Good water."

She bent down and drank for a long time. At last she sat up. "Good water," she signed again. And it was.

It started getting dark very quickly then. We all circled to the front of the shed, but something wasn't right. Something I could sense.

There was a smell inside the shed, a smell I recognized and didn't like. I tensed instinctively, and so did Roger beside me; as our eyes got used to the dim light, we could see Tarzan inside, curled up on a mat.

I looked around uncertainly. I *could* curl up in the opposite corner, and just hope he wouldn't get crazy. I glanced at Roger. He didn't even see me; he was busy staring at Tarzan. One look told me that his mind was made up, and then mine was, too. My hair bristled, I grunted angrily. Tarzan, taking up a space in *our* house! He jerked awake and sprang to his feet; he stared in surprise. Roger and I stood our ground, glaring back at him. Like giants, we pulled ourselves up to our full heights, rocking slowly back and forth. Roger hooted deep in his throat. For a moment, Tarzan faced us. Then he gave a scared, angry look, pushed between us, and scampered out into the jungle.

We went inside and sat down on our mats. Nibbles hesitated a moment, looking first after Tarzan and then, apprehensively, at us. Finally she came in and sat down, too.

We had taken possession of the shed. I wondered if it would be much protection against cannibals.

❦ 6 ❦
Midnight

I was hanging upside down, swaying, rocking side to side with each step, clinging to the chest-hair of the big female chimp who carried me. Her smell was familiar and reassuring: a chimp smell, certainly, but not threatening. Around us were other chimps, some giving food grunts as they ate a fruit I didn't recognize, some resting in the shade, some younger ones chasing each other in play. The big female chimp walked with me through a jungle. In my mind was a thought without words: I've been here before, I've clung to this chest, lived in this jungle. I looked up to the chimp who carried me: I trusted her. I trusted her. But I couldn't see her face. And somehow, there was nothing I wanted more in the whole world. It felt like the saddest thing I'd ever known: I kept looking up trying to see her, but I could never see her face. . . .

I woke up with a start. It was nighttime. I could make out the walls of the shed and the shapes of Nibbles and Roger lying on the dirt floor. The images of the big female chimp and the other jungle faded from my mind; only the sadness remained, a sadness I could now hardly remember the reason for. A *hoo*-sound rose in my throat; in the nighttime quiet it seemed to fill the whole shed, loud beyond my control. I struggled to hold it in; surely Roger and Nibbles would hear me, and they'd know, they'd know I was crying! Roger turned but didn't waken; and the rustling, sliding sound of his turning nearly made me jump, drowning out the sound within me. So. It wasn't loud, my sound, except to me; at least there was that. I let the sound out now, *hoo* after wave of *hoo*, until there was no more sound within me. And no one heard. No one at all.

After that I felt quieter.

I lay where I was and listened: the deep, slow breathing of Roger; Nibble's quicker, shallower breaths; the breeze in the leaves overhead. And then something different, sharper, somewhere out beyond the wall!

I sat up quickly; the moonlight hit me full in the

face, so bright I almost had to squint. It was quiet again. I held my breath and listened for what seemed like hours; my heart pounded. It was gone, whatever it was. I let my breath out. And there it was again, even closer!

"Nibbles!" I tugged at her shoulder; she opened an eye sleepily. "What was that?" I signed.

She sat up halfway.

"What was what?"

"That noise—didn't you hear it?"

"I was sleeping," she signed in the moonlight.

"Oh." I scanned the trees in front of us. "I hope it's not a lion!"

Nibbles sat up fully and hugged her knees to her chest. "Do you think it is?"

"I don't know. I—"

"Or the cannibals! Maybe it's the cannibals!"

My heart beat wildly. Cannibals—that should have been the first thing I thought of! What if—? I stopped myself. "No, this sounded too big for a cannibal."

"Do you really think there's a lion out there?"

My heart slowed, and suddenly I felt foolish. But it helped to know that she was up.

"There *was*." I listened a moment. "I don't know. I don't hear anything now."

"You think he's gone?"

I listened again; Roger grunted in his sleep in the

62

corner and turned on his side. Then everything was quiet.

I nodded.

"What'll we do if he comes back?"

"I don't know. Maybe he won't find us."

"Oh." Nibbles looked down at her hands.

"You scared?"

She nodded.

"Ever been away from home before?"

"No. Have you?"

"No." I thought a moment. "Yeah. I guess so."

"Don't you know?"

"I mean, a long time ago. They said I was born in Africa. I used to live in a place like this."

She looked at me with a little more respect. "Then I guess you're used to it."

"Kind of." I let out my breath. "Guess the lion won't bother us tonight."

"You sure?"

"I don't know." I listened again. "Yeah. I guess I'm sure."

I started to lie down again. Nibbles tugged at my hand. "Danny?"

"Yeah?"

"Do you think we'll ever get home again?"

I hesitated a moment. "Yeah. I think so."

"But what if we don't?"

"I don't know. We'll get out."

"But what if we *don't*?"

I didn't know what to answer, and I wished she wouldn't keep asking and making me think about it. I rubbed my ear uncomfortably.

"I drank the water," she signed at last.

"I know. So did I."

"But I *drank* it. Daddy said no. He *always* said no: Don't drink from ground, drink from cup."

"Your daddy isn't here now. And neither is your cup."

"But Daddy said—"

"I know what your daddy said." I looked her in the eye. "But he didn't say it *here*."

"But—"

"Listen to me, Nibbles. You could pretend it's like you're still back at home. You could refuse to drink the water. You could do everything your daddy ever told you. And you'd starve to death in no time. 'Don't drink dirty,' 'Don't eat from ground.' I know: Daddy said." I grunted angrily. "*Your* daddy said, *my* daddy said, *Roger's* daddy said. They all said lots of things. But they should have said one thing more: *Forget* everything Daddy said, 'cause Daddy's shipping you off to some grungy, flea-bitten old island where nothing Daddy said makes sense anymore." I paused. "They could have said that. They could have at *least* done that for us." I swallowed; then I spat outside the shed to hide what I was feeling. "They probably never even thought of it."

Nibbles watched me awhile without moving. Then she dropped her eyes and started making small movements with her hands, one sign over and over. "Daddy. Daddy. Daddy."

I touched her shoulder. She looked up at me.

"You think we'll be here a long time," she signed.

I didn't answer.

"You said I could starve. It takes a long time to starve. You think we might be here a long time."

"I don't know." I paused. "I just don't know."

"If they . . ." She looked quickly down and stopped signing. "If they leave us," she signed at last, "if they leave us here, then they'll never know." Her eyes opened in astonishment as the thought fully dawned on her. "They won't know what we're doing; they won't even know if we're signing anymore." Her face twisted. "I could learn a hundred new signs, *and they'd never even know.*"

I felt a kind of twinge, an emptiness in the pit of my stomach.

She swallowed. "If they leave us, do you think maybe they'll come back someday? And we can show them then?"

"*I* don't know! Do you think they even care? Do you think they've even given us a second thought, now that they've gotten rid of us?"

She stared at me in silence. And I knew I'd made a mistake. I'd needed her to be there, needed her awake. And now I was making her feel like *that*.

She signed to herself in small movements. "Daddy cares, Daddy will come back, Daddy cares." She looked up at me. "But why Daddy doesn't come? Why Daddy doesn't take me back?"

Another question I couldn't answer. "I don't know," I signed. I wished there were something more I could say to her.

She sat quietly for a while. The wind rustled through the palm leaves. Roger snored and threw an arm over his face.

"Danny," she signed at last. "Will you help protect us and teach us how to live in the jungle—I mean, if we have to?"

"If we have to," I signed quickly. "Sure. I can do that."

"Thank you."

I was suddenly sleepy again, as sleepy as I'd ever been in my life. I started to turn on my side, but she tapped me on the back.

"Danny, were you *very* little when they took you from the jungle?"

"Oh—um, I don't remember, I—"

"What?"

"They said I was pretty little."

She knitted her brows in concern. "But then you couldn't—"

"Well, "not *that* little," I lied.

"Oh." She breathed more easily. "I'm glad you can teach us." She rested her chin on her hand; she seemed to be thinking. "Is there really a lion here?" she signed at last.

I thought for a moment. "I don't think so," I signed.

"Then I don't think there's a lion, either." She sighed. "Daddy will come. Tomorrow. Daddy will come tomorrow."

I nodded.

"Good night, Danny."

She rolled onto her tummy, and in a moment she was breathing heavily. I watched her.

"Good night, Nibbles," I signed even though she couldn't see me.

Somehow she seemed even smaller when she was sleeping. I let my eyes close, too.

In a moment, the big female chimp was carrying me through the jungle again. She carried me till morning.

❧ 7 ❧
We Take
Our Chance

The sun shone brightly in my eyes. I woke up slowly, reaching for the covers to pull over my head. But there weren't any covers. I reached to pick them up from the floor, stretching over where the edge of the bed should have been. But there wasn't any edge, either, and I scraped my hand against the dirt! I tried to focus. *This wasn't my room. Where was I?* I felt a panicky feeling in my stomach. Then I made out the walls of the shed and the trees outside the opening, and it all came back to me. I was really here, on Chimp Island; it was really true. I felt so lost I wanted to cry. But there was Roger sitting near the open end of the shed grooming himself, and there was Nibbles lying next to me, and I was afraid they'd see.

I started to sit up, but my back felt as if someone had just pulled it out like Turkish taffy. Every muscle ached. I lay down again.

"Nice day," signed Roger and again combed his fingers through the long, dark hair of his leg. "It's getting hot already."

I didn't respond.

Roger gave me a funny look. "Good morning, Danny. Where is your head?"

"What?"

"Well, I saw your routine on *Sixty Minutes*. Just trying to make you feel at home."

"Very funny."

I turned away, but Roger circled in front of me. "Where is your nose? Where are your fingers? Where is your belly button? Where is your ear?" I didn't answer. "All right, where is *my* ear?"

"It'll be hanging from my teeth, if you don't lay off!"

"My, my!" Roger smiled.

Nibbles slowly opened her eyes and looked around, then buried her head in the mat again.

All at once, a sputtering sound in the distance got loud and suddenly stopped, and I realized I'd been hearing it for some time. The motorboat, down at the beach! Roger recognized it the same moment I did. We'd meant to get up early and plan before Dr. Simeon got here. But we hadn't counted on how tired we were from our trip, and now it was too late. Dr. Simeon was back already, and we still didn't have a plan!

Next came the unmistakable sound of Tarzan screeching. I tore out of the shed and ran down the path, with Roger and Nibbles close behind. I didn't know what we'd do when we found Dr. Simeon, but I knew we couldn't let a chance go by.

Down on the beach, Tarzan was pulling at Dr. Simeon's pants, dragging him over to show him something. He paused for just a second when he heard us coming, and then pulled even harder, as if he were afraid that Dr. Simeon would desert him for us.

"All right, Tarzan!" Dr. Simeon was signing as he stumbled along under Tarzan's pull. "I'm coming, I'm coming! What's so important?"

Tarzan pulled him a little way more, then stopped and grunted. In front of him lay two stones, one piled on top of the other. The top stone was a round one, half Tarzan's size; I could tell from the tracks that he'd dragged it from halfway across the beach. The bottom one was large and wedge-shaped. At the four corners of the wedge, he'd placed four smaller, round stones. Tarzan pointed and grunted some more as if all this were supposed to mean something —all the while looking from Dr. Simeon to the stones and back again, to be sure that Dr. Simeon was looking.

I stared. Was this what Tarzan *had* to show him?

Dr. Simeon gave him a puzzled look. "Yes, Tarzan?"

Tarzan pointed again and grunted more insistently.

"Uh, yes, I see, Tarzan. You did that all by yourself? That's wonderful, Tarzan, wonderful!"

He turned to go, but Tarzan grabbed him by the pants again and grunted loudly. It almost sounded like a threat. Then he sat down facing the stones and started pounding with his fingers on the wedge. It was the same strange sign he had made yesterday.

"Tarzan," signed Dr. Simeon, "why don't you just try *signing* what you have to tell me?"

Tarzan gave a strangled-sounding grunt and pounded at the wedge even more frantically.

Dr. Simeon turned to Brian. "I guess it must be a stress reaction, right? He's regressing to earlier modes of behavior."

Tarzan screamed and slapped at the wedge. For a moment the large round stone rocked at the top; then it tottered and started rolling, straight for Tarzan! And the looney wasn't even watching. He was just looking at Dr. Simeon. Nibbles screamed, and Tarzan jumped to the side—an instant before the stone rolled by him.

Tarzan scurried a few steps away, then got his courage back and inspected the damage. He made a half-hearted effort to roll the round stone up the wedge again, at the same time giving Dr. Simeon an accusing look, as if to say, "What's the use?" Finally he pounded his forehead and shrieked. The way he was carrying on, you'd think his life's work had been destroyed.

"Tarzan, Tarzan," signed Dr. Simeon. "You can build another one."

Tarzan hopelessly repeated his finger-jabbing sign in the sand. Then he buried his head in his arms.

Dr. Simeon shook his head; it took him a few moments before he could put his happy everything-under-control face on again.

"Good morning!" He turned to Nibbles, Roger, and me.

"Good morning," we signed back.

Dr. Simeon brightened and raised his eyebrows significantly to Brian. I knew that look, from Dr. Franklin. It meant, more or less, "Look! See what progress they're making!" And the dumb jerk was taking credit for it, too.

"Did you find your shed last night?"

"Yes," I signed.

72

"Good!" Dr. Simeon smiled.

"Yes." Nibbles got her courage up. "But it's not a nice house. Not nice!"

I looked at Nibbles in surprise. I didn't think she'd have the courage to say it. Roger and I nodded and grunted, to back her up.

"Oh." Dr. Simeon wrinkled his forehead; it was his concerned look. "I'm sorry you feel that way. You see, we built this for you all by ourselves, and this was all we could—"

"It's small and dirty!" I broke in.

"There's no floor!" signed Nibbles. "And no door! And there are holes in the wall!"

"It stinks!" I signed.

"Oh." Dr. Simeon licked his lips. "Well, you see, this is only temporary. Actually we *could* have built something more like what you're used to—"

"Then why didn't you?" I interrupted.

"Excuse me, Danny. As I was saying, we *could* have done that, but we wanted you to get used to the idea of living in nature—you know, sleeping under the stars, nesting in trees, living just like the chimps in Africa. So we felt that the shed could remind you a little of home but still get you into the right spirit."

We stared. Dr. Simeon took a breath. "I'll try to say it more simply. You see—"

"Yeah, sure," I signed, "we see. We're just animals, so we should be happy sleeping on a dirty mat on the floor."

"Well, no really, it's not that—I . . ." Dr. Simeon stumbled. "Roger, *you* must understand what I'm saying."

Roger nodded. "Yes, I do understand."

"Thank you."

"I had hoped you would have had enough respect for us to provide more suitable quarters."

Dr. Simeon did a doubletake, and then looked as if he had to stop himself from bursting out laughing, as if he thought it was hysterical to be addressed that way by a chimp. But the three of us just stared at him in dead earnest. The smile faded, and his face got red.

"I'm sorry," he signed clumsily. "I'll see what can be done."

"Yes," signed Roger, "do that."

"Well . . ." Dr. Simeon tried to brighten the atmosphere. "Did you find the fruit trees?"

I gave him a blank look. "Fruit trees?"

"Yes, that's one of the things that are so nice about Chimp Island: lots and lots of fruit trees, with lots and lots of fruit!"

Roger seemed to pick up on my game. He looked puzzled. "We saw many trees . . ." he signed.

"But fruit comes from the refrigerator," I continued for him.

74

"Or from the bucket," signed Roger.

Brian rolled his eyes, but Dr. Simeon just smiled.

"Well, I can see we'll have to show you!" Dr. Simeon adjusted his safari helmet. "Follow me!"

Dr. Simeon started along the path, with me and Nibbles and Roger behind. Brian brought up the rear, and Tarzan tagged along some distance behind the lot of us.

"There!" After a short distance, Dr. Simeon pointed in triumph. "There's a coconut tree!"

"Yes, this *is* a tree," signed Roger doubtfully.

"But where are the coconuts?" I continued.

"Right up there!" signed Dr. Simeon. "See? At the top of the tree."

"Oh, yes!" I signed. "Please you get them for us?"

Dr. Simeon skipped a beat. "Why, you can get them yourselves. All you have to do is climb the tree!"

Roger and I exchanged innocent glances. "Climb?"

"You mean you never climbed trees when you went to the park or playground?"

We shook our heads.

Dr. Simeon looked at us closely. "Are you sure?"

Brian rolled his eyes again. He wasn't being taken in.

I turned all my attention to Dr. Simeon. "Please, you show us?"

Dr. Simeon didn't answer.

"You see," Roger interjected, "you have to under-stand: We were brought up in cities and in laboratories. We never learned the usual survival skills."

"You show us, please?" I repeated.

Dr. Simeon took a breath. "Brian," he said at last, "show them how to climb a tree."

"What!" Brian hit the roof.

"Well . . ."

Brian pulled Dr. Simeon a short distance away, and they exchanged angry whispers. I only caught a little of it, but I didn't have to hear much to figure out what was going on. Brian was telling Dr. Simeon that he was letting a bunch of chimps make a monkey out of him, and Dr. Simeon was saying, well, yes, maybe, but then again, maybe we were telling the truth. At last Dr. Simeon broke the huddle and walked back to us.

"Nibbles," he signed, fixing her with a gaze. Nibbles had been fidgeting and doing her best to pretend that she was somewhere else ever since Roger and I had started our game. Now she was afraid to meet Dr. Simeon's eyes.

"Nibbles," he repeated. "Listen to me. I've heard that you're a very good girl and that you never ever tell lies. Is that right?"

She nodded.

"Good. I know you are. Now tell me the truth, Nibbles. Do you and your friends know how to climb a tree?"

76

Nibbles looked at Dr. Simeon—a helpless look, almost begging to be excused from answering—then stole a glance at us; I signaled her with a tiny "no" shake of my head. She turned quickly away and back to Dr. Simeon. She seemed almost paralyzed.

"Nibbles, tell me: Can you and your friends climb trees?"

Nibbles looked at the ground and swallowed. Then, with the tiniest movement of her hands, she signed, "No."

"What was that?" asked Dr. Simeon.

"No!" she repeated with a larger movement.

Dr. Simeon nodded. "Thank you, Nibbles. Brian, show them how to climb a tree."

Brian tore his hat off and threw it to the ground, muttering furiously under his breath. Then he picked out a fairly small tree and started shimmying up the trunk—slipping and huffing and puffing and grunting, and looking like the silliest human being I've ever seen. Then the three of us had to give it a try. We did it as clumsily as we could, but even so we weren't nearly as bad as Brian. Tarzan refused to understand or else refused to try. He just sat in the path, watching us with a strange expression on his face. Roger and I got halfway up, then slid down and asked Brian to show us again. By the time he was finished, his shirt was torn and his face was covered with dirt; he pursed his lips and gave me an ugly look.

"You must forgive us," Roger signed after a number of tries. "These are new skills for us. We must still learn many lessons in how to gather food, if we are to survive."

"Yes," I signed. "I'm afraid we'll need you here to teach us for many days."

Dr. Simeon nodded grimly. Brian glared down from his perch at Dr. Simeon and us. I couldn't tell whether he was angrier at Dr. Simeon or at Roger and me. Roger and I somehow managed to keep from laughing, but Nibbles sat looking at her hands and from time to time let out a soft, forlorn, "Hoo."

All at once, Brian noticed Nibbles again, and something seemed to click in his mind. I'd seen the expression on his face a few times before, usually just before he came up with something new to try on me in the laboratory. It meant that he had an idea. And Brian's ideas were never good news.

"Nibbles," he signed. "You've hardly tried it at all."

Nibbles looked at him out of the corner of her eye and then looked down at her hands again.

"Why, yes," he continued. "I saw you, and you only climbed once. Why don't you give it another try?"

He climbed about halfway down, casually picking something I couldn't quite make out from a branch and sticking it in his pocket; then he half-jumped, half-slipped to the ground, scraping himself all over again. He picked himself up and stood right in front of Nibbles. He touched her on the shoulder.

"Your turn again." He looked right at her. "Climb."

Nibbles could climb all right. And she'd shown that she could lie, with difficulty, when she had to. But could she pretend that she *couldn't* climb, with Brian standing practically on top of her—and make him believe her?

"Climb," he repeated.

Nibbles looked to me, then to Dr. Simeon, then back to Brian again.

"You can do it." He gave her a reassuring pat that made my skin crawl. "We'll do it together."

He took her by the hand and pulled gently. She stood up. He led her toward an easy climbing tree; she hung back, looking to me again, but Brian was firm.

"There we go. One foot here, one foot here." He helped her put her feet on either side of a low fork in the trunk. "That's it. Hands here. And now we hold on and take a step." He slipped, then caught himself and made it to the next foothold. He seemed to be getting the hang of things a little more now, and so did Nibbles. "*Very* good!" He smiled. "Are you *sure* you've never done this before?"

They were getting higher now, step by step. Nibbles kept looking to me and back to Brian again. She didn't play her part the way Roger and I did;

her footing was sure, and there was none of the slipping and sliding that Roger and I had done. But she did take it slowly, and at least she wasn't obvious about her climbing experience. Maybe it would still be okay.

"Now a little higher."

I looked to Dr. Simeon. He was watching closely, his forehead wrinkled with concern. "Brian, do you really think—"

"She's doing fine," said Brian. He and Nibbles climbed a little more.

"That's the idea." Brian hoisted himself just behind her and pulled something skinny from his pocket. He brushed the bottom of her foot with it as she took a step, then quickly dropped it to the ground before she could look.

"Nibbles, look out!" he signed. "Wasn't that a snake?"

Nibbles jerked back in terror, almost losing her footing. She found it again in an instant and clambered up the tree, branch after branch, her lips drawn back in fright. She was too far now, out toward the skinny end of the branch. It bent beneath her, groaning and creaking with her weight. And still she kept going, glancing in panic over her shoulder for pursuing snakes. Then there was a cracking sound, and she tumbled from on top, still gripping tight with her hands. She stayed like that for a long, frozen moment, screeching and hanging from the bobbing branch.

Dr. Simeon circled beneath her, looking almost as terror-stricken as Nibbles. He ran back and forth with gaping eyes, open mouth, outstretched hands —and not the slightest idea of what to do.

Then the branch gave the cracking sound again.

The excitement was too much. I felt myself begin to panic, just as Nibbles had, and for no good reason. But I couldn't stop it. Tarzan was hooting with excitement, and so was I. Then Nibbles gave a danger cry. That sound did it. I told myself to stop and think, but I couldn't stop, and I couldn't think at all: the danger cry seemed to cut through everything, everything I knew or could control. Before I knew it, I was scurrying up the tree next to Nibbles's, almost flying to the end of a branch. Without stopping, I grabbed the next branch and swung breathless into Nibbles's tree, just as she swung to mine. Then the next branch, and the next, then into the tree next to that one. We couldn't stop, and we couldn't have done it better if we'd practiced.

I didn't stop till I was safely at the top of a straight tree with broad, thick leaves. Nibbles's danger cries turned to whimpers. I caught my breath and felt my heart slow. I could think again now. And all at once, I almost wished I couldn't. I looked down and all around me. And I knew we were in trouble.

Tarzan was sitting again, not doing much of anything. Dr. Simeon was standing and looking up at
me in amazement. And Brian was looking from me
to Nibbles to Dr. Simeon with a smile I knew well
and didn't like. I looked down to Roger, but he
didn't see me; he was just covering his eyes and
shaking his head, wincing as if he couldn't bear to
see what had just happened. I didn't wait for his
eyes to meet mine; I looked up toward the treetops,
hoping I'd never have to look at anyone.

"Danny!" Brian called. I looked down at him.
"That was some pretty fancy climbing."

I grabbed the first thing I could find and threw it
at him. It was a banana.

Brian dodged. "Dr. Simeon!" He laughed. "Would
you call that aggression or food-gathering behavior?"

He felt so proud, I wanted to bean him. But Roger
gave me a warning grunt, and I realized he was
right. I probably couldn't make things any better,
but at least I could keep from making them worse.

"*Very* nice climbing," Brian repeated.

"Scared," I signed. "Scared."

"I know you were. But, just the same, today wasn't
the first time you climbed a tree—was it, Nibbles?"

Nibbles looked down at her hands.

"Nibbles," he called. She looked at him. "It's okay
now. The snake is gone."

" 'Snake.' " Roger got up and walked to the base

82

of the tree. He picked up the skinny thing that Brian had dropped. It was a twig. "Here's your 'snake.' "

Nibbles's eyes got wide.

Brian smiled.

Nibbles looked from the twig to Brian, her face filled with disbelief. At last she signed.

"You said there was a snake."

"There could have been."

"You—you *lied* to me!"

"But, Nibbles"—he looked up to her—"you lied to us *first*."

I couldn't help myself: I threw another banana, hitting Brian square on the chest with a satisfying thud. He jerked his head up at me and seemed to take a minute to get his breath back. Then he stepped carefully behind a tree and out of my range.

"Well, Brian," Dr. Simeon said at last, "I hate to say it, but it looks as if you were right after all."

Brian shrugged. "It wasn't me. It was the committee; it's what they've been saying all along."

"Yes. And you've been pointing out to me the wisdom of their view."

Brian nodded. "I mean, of course, it's up to you. If you want, we could stay down here for months and play nursemaid to them, the way they do at Baboon Island . . ."

"No, you're right, Brian. It would only inhibit their natural adjustment to the new environment."

I gave Roger a questioning look.

"He said, we'll learn quicker if they just leave us here alone now," Roger explained.

"Alone?"

"*Really* alone."

My stomach turned upside down.

"And after your demonstration," Roger continued, "it's a bit hard to argue with them."

❧ 8 ❧
Alone

Brian and Dr. Simeon gathered their things pretty quickly. I heard them talking, saying something about "coordinating" in New York and how the committee's approach deserved "a chance." And Dr. Simeon said, more than once, that the best thing they could do for us right now was to let us "work things out" for ourselves for a while—apparently a pretty long while—before checking back on us. It didn't sound like the best thing to me.

As they shouldered their last piece of equipment, I scampered down from my tree and ran up to them on all fours. I looked up to Dr. Simeon but didn't sign anything; I just watched him, letting the look say it all. Then Tarzan approached, as close as he dared with the rest of us there, and gave him the same worried look of appeal. Dr. Simeon turned away, but I followed him, and Tarzan did also, at a distance. Dr. Simeon walked a little farther, trying to avoid looking at us; we continued in his footsteps. Finally, he turned back and faced us.

"You'll be okay," he signed. "I promise, you guys will be all right." But he didn't look us in the eye.

We didn't even try to stop them when they left this time. It seemed as if there was nothing left to say. Except to ask them when they'd be back again. And I didn't have the courage for that.

I climbed back into my tree and didn't come down again until midafternoon; neither did Nibbles. I finally did when I got hungry, and walked to the beach.

The styrofoam bucket was gone. Half a bologna and cheese sandwich was sitting on the beach where it had fallen, almost covered with sand. I tried it and gagged. I was spitting sand out of my mouth for the rest of the day.

I couldn't stay on the beach long. The sun baked my skin, and the air was so heavy I could hardly breathe. I needed some shade.

I went back to the trees and picked up one of the bananas I'd pelted at Brian. It was a little green and hard, but it was food. I ate half of it.

"Ah, the natural diet." Roger stepped out from behind a tree where he had been resting. "Plucked from the trees by your own natural knowhow."

I was going to sign something back to him when I heard a sound overhead. At first I didn't see anything. Then I saw something small like a bird that flashed sunlight and got bigger and louder as it got closer. It was the plane that had brought us here. And it was landing on the mainland.

I looked at Roger, and I looked up at Nibbles in the tree. Her eyes were wide and scared, and I guess mine were, too; even Roger looked shaken. And on a ridge up the hillside, I could see Tarzan watching; the look on his face was the most hopeless of all. We were still for a long time. Then, on the faraway mainland, the plane took off again, undoubtedly taking Brian and Dr. Simeon with it, for who knew how long. We looked at each other; there was just nothing to say.

I looked back at Roger; he was the last thing I wanted to deal with. I walked away into the bushes and lay down where no one could see me. And there I stayed the rest of the day, watching the black, heavy clouds in the distance. I didn't climb back to the shed until after sunset.

The thunder broke some time in the middle of the night. The wind stirred up, sweeping through the branches overhead; then came the patter of raindrops on the leaves and the roof. In no time, the patter was a pounding. Lightning flashed, and thunder cracked so loud I jumped. The roof and walls leaked; a torrent of water spouted from a corner of the roof and spread over the floor, soaking the mats. Nibbles and I huddled together miserably, trying and failing to keep clear of the dirty puddles. Even Roger had no ideas. He sat by the opening, leaning forward tensely, watching what he could see of the surrounding trees with each flash of lightning.

All at once the wind ripped even stronger. Cold rain pelted me like ice balls; the boards groaned, and for one awful moment I thought the whole shed would be blown away. Then we wouldn't have even that, miserable as it was. We'd have no shelter at all. Like Tarzan. The wind died down again, and I caught my breath.

I hadn't meant to think of him—of Tarzan, I mean. I wondered what he was doing now. Well, he could find some trees or something to hide under. Whatever he was using, it couldn't be much worse than what we had. Not a *lot* worse, anyway.

The rain finally stopped around dawn, and I dropped off into a shivery sleep. All in all, it was the longest night of my life.

It wasn't the sunlight that woke me in the morning. And it wasn't the sound of the birds all waking up and calling to each other from the trees all around us. It wasn't even the scraping sound and tugging feeling as Roger pulled out the soaking mats and laid them in the sun to dry, tumbling me into a dirty puddle. It was the emptiness in my stomach that woke me, a gnawing ache that seemed to get worse with each rumble.

"Well, Danny," Roger signed after giving a final yank to pull the mat out from under me, "I suppose you *could* just stay in there till you rot; and at the moment, I probably wouldn't be overwhelmed with grief if you did. But it might be wiser to get out into the sun. You need to get warm and dry."

I *needed* a nice warm bath and my Columbia sweatshirt and my own warm bed and a big plate of scrambled eggs and a steaming cup of hot chocolate and three slices of toast with butter and lots of grape jelly, that was what I *needed*. I turned on my side, groaning at the effort, and faced the wall. I'd thought my muscles had ached yesterday, but this was ridiculous. I felt as if I'd never move again.

"Danny." Roger was leaning over me. "I said *out*." The words were so familiar it could have been Dr. Franklin almost any morning. I must be having a bad dream. *"Now!"* He gave me a yank that made my arm feel like it had been pulled out of my shoulder.

"Leave me alone!" I signed.

"Move, Danny!" He prepared to give me another expert yank.

I staggered up and out of the shed. "What's it to you?" I signed sloppily as I lay down in the sun next to Nibbles.

Roger stood looking at the two of us and shook his head. I drifted off again.

"What is it to me?" Roger signed when I opened my eyes again. Even after his morning grooming, he still looked a sorry sight: his hair bedraggled, his face grim and determined. "What's it to me?" He shrugged. "Oh, nothing really. Just a little matter of survival for all of us, that's all. As much as you dislike thinking about that little question, it suddenly does seem to have become priority number one, thanks in large part to the actions of certain chimps who will be nameless. That's 'what it is to me.'" He pressed his lips in a thin, hard line. "And, much as I hate to say it, we'll stand our best chance working together."

I tried to sit up and almost made it. My eyes blurred, then focused again.

"And right now that means work"—he grunted in emphasis—"*specifically getting up and food-gathering. Now. This morning.* Yes, I'm sore; yes, I'd like to take the day off, too. But we need food right now. And if we don't go out and get it today, we'll be even weaker tomorrow. I'm sorry if that's upsetting to anyone, but it happens to be the case." His eyes scanned the two of us. He breathed slowly.

"And as for this morning"—his eyes flashed—"don't you *ever* leave it all to me again. Everyone uses his head, everyone works, everyone gets his own unlovely carcass up in the morning, or I make it on my own. Understood?"

I thought of telling him he couldn't talk to me that way, but this morning I didn't have the strength to argue. Or even to resent it very much. I let it pass.

"Well, I think the point is made." His eyes returned to their usual mildness. "And, speaking solely for myself, I think some breakfast would be the first order for survival."

My stomach gave a loud rumble. I'd have given anything for a good breakfast. But the thought of the kind of effort we'd needed yesterday . . .

"How will we get it?" I signed.

Roger just looked at me, deadpan, as if to say, "How do you think?"

I groaned. "But I can't climb today. I just can't!" I made a pathetic effort to stand up, then sank back to my knees again.

Roger regarded me drily. "You should have been that convincing yesterday," he signed. "After all, you *are* supposed to be an actor, or so I thought."

For once he was right. If they could see us now, they'd *never* just leave us.

I was past trying. The best I could do was imagine. I pictured mountains of blueberry pancakes floating in a lake of maple syrup and melted butter. In my mind, I piled a bunch of raisins and banana slices on top of the pancakes, along with nuts and an ice cream scoop and half a Mars bar for good measure. As long as I was imagining, I might as well do it all the way, and I added whipped cream and a maraschino cherry on top. My stomach growled hopelessly, and I felt like crying. I never thought I could be so weak and so hungry at the same time! I could see myself eating the pancakes now, slurping up the ice cream, mashing the bananas. . . . My stomach gave another unbearable pang. I thought of starving to death while just sitting there imagining breakfast, and I knew I couldn't let it happen that way.

"I guess I can walk a little," I signed at last.

"Glad to hear it, Danny. That's a start."

Nibbles signed for the first time. "But climbing. . . !"

She was right. My leg muscles were knotted like a rope; even walking was a heroic effort.

Roger spat. "Well then— any bright ideas, anyone?"

The wind blew through the branches softly, showering us with droplets from last night's rain— and with one stray leaf. And all at once I did have an idea. Not a brilliant one, but practical enough, just the same.

"Nibbles, maybe we won't *have* to climb."

"We won't?"

"After that storm last night, I'll bet there's plenty of fruit right on the ground, if we know where to look for it."

A startled expression came over Roger's face for just an instant, and then it was gone again.

"Well, Danny, I see you *can* use your head when you need to, at least for the obvious thoughts."

The idea *was* pretty obvious. But somehow Roger had missed it, I was almost sure. Probably he was too busy playing boss to even think of it. *I'd thought of it, and Roger hadn't.* And what Roger had meant as an insult was not far from the truth: I *could* use my head, and even get some ideas that Roger might miss. And knowing that, made Roger a little more bearable. After all, I could use *my* head, too. We started down the path.

Even Roger wasn't much good on his feet that morning. If he had had to climb a tree, he probably would somehow have managed it, just through sheer willpower. But I think even he was glad not to have to do it. The three of us hobbled along on the easiest paths, keeping a lookout for coconuts and bananas and any other fruits that had been knocked down by the storm. We followed our noses, almost fainting from hunger at the overpowering, sweet smell as we neared our goal. We remembered where some of the heaviest fruit bunches had been hanging yesterday, and sure enough, a few of them were toppled. We even found mangoes in a grove by the stream: dozens of them, ripe and juicy, just lying where they had fallen. At the first squirty, tart-sweet taste, my mouth revived and my stomach squeezed even tighter, and then I gave myself over to the moist sweetness. It was the best fruit I'd ever tasted.

We'd probably have to climb for our breakfast on other mornings; with some rest—*lots* of rest—and conditioning, I hoped we could manage it. But today, when we'd really needed it, the food had been within our reach. The island had helped us.

❧ 9 ❧
Survival

As the days went by, we learned to find the island's fruit; and as our muscles got used to the routine, we climbed for our food. Little by little, we were getting used to finding our way around on the island —or, more precisely, on our half of it. We kept well away from the hillside where we'd seen the cannibal tracks. Roger reminded us more than once of the danger, but he didn't have to bother: Nibbles and I remembered it well enough.

Tarzan, as far as we knew, never explored that way either; and after the first day, he kept pretty much to himself. He seemed to spend most of his time sitting on a ridge, looking out to sea, apparently watching for the return of Brian and Dr. Simeon. Sometimes I'd see him practicing his strange finger-jabbing sign on the ground as he looked out toward the horizon with a hopeless expression on his face.

We got some of our strength back after that first day, but not all of it. And every one of us was hungering, craving, for something besides fruit. Even the mangoes lost their appeal. It wasn't so much the Mars bars and thick shakes that I craved; I missed them. sure, my mouth watered when I thought of them. But at night I *dreamed* of hamburgers, of fried chicken, even of foods I'd hated like liver and string beans—as Roger said, we missed our protein and fresh vegetables. But they weren't as easy to come by as the fruits. And even Roger hesitated to try foods he didn't know.

Soon a strange thing happened: within days, we seemed to be getting weaker again. Even walking became an effort. We practically dragged ourselves through the forest, and Nibbles was sniffling much of the day. I felt in my gut that I needed something more than fruit to eat, but I couldn't bring myself to do it.

One morning we dragged ourselves up a small hill we'd climbed easily only a few days before. We stood panting at the top, and I think we all knew that something had to be done. I looked at Roger, and he looked back at me.

"Weren't you the one, just a few days ago, who was talking about living on leaves and bark? And how charming that would be?"

He smiled wryly. "You know I was."

"And how we all had to do new things and 'adapt' if we wanted to survive?"

He nodded.

"Well?"

He sighed. "I know, Danny. But then again, I *have* had a certain upbringing."

"So where do you think *we* were raised? Central Park? You old phoney." I sat down. "Nuts to you, Roger!"

He stood where he was for a long time without moving. At last he grunted. "Your point is well taken, Danny. Very well taken." With that he walked a short distance to a tree with broad leaves growing from an overhanging branch. It was one of the commonest trees on the island, one we passed lots of times every day; but never before had we eaten from it. This time Roger stopped, stared up, and studied the leaves; he seemed to be building up his will power. Finally, he reached up and tore off a few leaves, smelled them, and took a deep breath; then he put them in his mouth and chewed. I got up, and Nibbles and I crowded around to watch him; he seemed to consider for a moment, then swallowed and let out a satisfied food grunt. He munched another handful.

"Not the most delicate salad I've ever eaten," he signed at last, "but I think it will do."

I sniffed and inspected the leaves, and so did Nibbles. The idea of eating leaves from a tree still seemed strange: there was something in me that absolutely refused. But Roger had taken my challenge, and they seemed all right for him, so I couldn't chicken out. I waited a moment more and finally tore off part of a leaf and chewed it. It was tough, all right, and surprisingly bitter—somewhere between spinach and celery, only about four times stronger. I spit it out.

Roger smiled. "Doesn't quite compare with a Big Mac, does it?" He ate another handful.

I grimaced. If Roger could eat it, then so could I. And I wasn't about to give him any more advantages. I grabbed a small handful and forced myself to chew and swallow. No, it wasn't exactly a Big Mac—or even spinach or string beans—that was for sure. But it *was* food, and I could learn to eat it.

Over the next few days, we added other leaves and stems and even kinds of tree bark to our diet. Not everything we tried turned out to be something we could eat again. But we kept experimenting, and slowly I could feel some of my strength coming back. The foods were strange, and some of them at first tasted awful. But they seemed to fill an empty spot in my stomach.

Only Nibbles refused to try: she stuck to fruits alone. She continued to seem weak, and her cold didn't get any better, but she managed to get around, and after a while we stopped bothering her about it and let her eat what she wanted. We just couldn't worry about it.

Until the morning she didn't get out of the shed. At first we thought she was just sleepy, so we got up and gathered our food without her. But when we got back, she still hadn't moved; her eyes were open and watching us, but she wouldn't sit up. She just lay there, breathing heavily. And she stayed like that all morning.

A clammy fist seemed to tighten inside my stomach. I had no way of knowing exactly how sick she was. But she didn't look good, and I knew that if you got sick *enough*, you could die. And if Nibbles could die, then I could die, too. It wasn't the kind of thing I wanted to realize.

Then Nibbles gave a deep, rasping breath, and the thought jarred loose from my mind. I had one practical thing to worry about. And that was Nibbles. Nibbles needed help. And most probably food, the foods she wasn't eating. Nibbles needed to eat.

I tried almost everything, and so did Roger. We scolded her, we reasoned with her, we even brought her different foods and held them up to her mouth and showed her how we were eating them. But she just kept her mouth closed. Her sad eyes seemed to say that she wanted to obey us but simply couldn't. I knew how she felt; it had seemed like almost a physical obstacle between *me* and the new foods, too.

I finally dropped the leaves I'd brought her that morning. I just didn't know what else to do.

Then Roger stood over her.

"Nibbles, you have to eat," he signed.

She didn't answer.

"Nibbles."

She shook her head weakly.

Roger paced within the small space of the shed. Then he came back to her.

"Nibbles, do you remember your daddy?"

Of course she did. I wondered why he even asked.

"Do you remember the last time you saw him?"

She nodded.

"What happened?"

"He gave me a banana treat and hugged me."

"And what did he say?"

"You know what he said. I told you."

"Tell me again."

Her face twisted. "He said, 'Be a good girl and take care of yourself.' "

"And *is* Nibbles a good girl?"

She nodded.

"No." He regarded her solemnly. "Nibbles is not a good girl. Nibbles is a bad girl."

She opened her mouth in astonishment and outrage. "Nibbles is good! Nibbles is good!"

Roger shook his head. "No. Your daddy said, 'Take care of yourself.' But you're not eating what you need. You're not taking care of yourself."

"Nibbles is good. . . !" she repeated weakly.

"No." Roger looked at her. "Nibbles is bad."

She was quiet for a long time.

"Daddy wants me to eat?" she signed at last.

"Yes. Your daddy would want you to eat."

She looked at Roger, then down at the leaves, and finally picked one up and chewed on it. She ate limply and without expression—but she swallowed it.

It was days before Nibbles ventured very far from the shed again, and longer still before she moved with any kind of real energy. But little by little she got her strength back. In time she was swinging and climbing with Roger and me, determinedly if not yet eagerly, and eating the same foods we did. We'd had a close call, but we were all still alive.

We were getting used to the island in some ways, though it was hardly home. Every night I dreamed of Peggy and my own room and our games of hide-and-seek and of good breakfasts and dinners that Peggy set before me and of Peggy stroking my head and telling me welcome back and hugging me. I'd wake up with an ache in my throat that wouldn't go away. Sometimes I'd hear Nibbles whimpering in her sleep. I assumed she was dreaming about her daddy; and in the mornings often she was very quiet and far away. Even Roger twitched and groaned in his sleep from time to time; I wondered what if anything *he* was dreaming about, but with Roger you never knew. In the daytime we put those thoughts away. They weren't any help, and we had lots to think about and learn just to keep going. But the thoughts of home were never *far* away. They were like a gray cloud hanging over us. I knew we should be thinking of a plan to use *if* Dr. Simeon and Brian should ever come back again and give us a chance to use it. But I really had no ideas. Just staying alive was taking up nearly all my energy.

We spent most of our days wandering through the forest, looking for food. It wasn't hard work, but it kept us busy. Roger usually got the most of any food that was near him. He talked about being civilized and needing each other; but when it came to food, he took what he could, with enthusiasm, and we learned not to challenge him or get in his way. Nibbles and I had to either range farther afield or wait till Roger was done in order to get our share. But he also had the sharpest eyes and the best feel for where a tasty treat might be, so it paid for us to stick with him. And, for whatever reason, he did keep us together and encourage us to keep going.

We were getting plenty of fruits and plants now. But we missed our meat. And every night, the hamburger that Peggy served me in my dream got bigger and juicier.

There were thoughts of other meat-eaters, too.

We could go for days almost believing that we were the only ones on the island, feeling like our half of the island was the only half there was. And then, at some quiet moment when we least expected it, the wind would shift and blow from the other side, and we'd suddenly hear faint hoots and food grunts. We froze, and each stole a glance toward Tarzan perching far away on his ridge. The sound hadn't come from him, and it hadn't come from us. It had come from the others, the ones we'd never seen. The cannibals.

I sometimes wondered how we could go so long without meeting them. I knew why *we* had never ventured to *their* side: we were terrified. But why had they never come to *us*? I thought of the thick underbrush we'd had to tear through that first day to get to the spot where we found the strange footprints. We'd barely made it through ourselves; perhaps, I thought gratefully, perhaps a chimp with the disadvantage of poles sticking through his feet couldn't make it at all.

Of course, there were lighter moments for us, too. And we needed them.

Nibbles had at first seemed kind of glassy-eyed and faraway after her sickness. But eventually she became playful. And I wasn't quite sure how to handle it.

One morning I was down by what Roger called the "staging area"—the spot where three hills face down toward a cave, like an outdoor theater. I was just resting after breakfast, when all of a sudden I heard a little rustle in the bushes. Before I knew it, someone was behind me, tickling me under the arms! I jumped up in panic, thinking of cannibals—and was halfway to a tree before I saw that it was only Nibbles. She was crouching in front of me now, panting a laugh, ready to run off a few steps and then scamper in and tickle me again. I looked at her in amazement and waved her off, but she came right back again with another attack, and another. I bared my teeth at her and grunted, but she just wouldn't quit, she kept running in and tickling me. And before I could stop myself, I was laughing and panting too, just the way I used to do with Peggy.

Soon we were playing and tickling almost every day. Sometimes we'd see Roger watching us with a strange expression on his face. I couldn't tell if he was looking down on us or wishing that he could join in, too. We did all three begin to join in on grooming sessions, running our fingers through each other's hair and picking insects from our bodies. But somehow I couldn't imagine Roger actually letting go and tickling with us. And he never did.

The one kind of game Roger joined in on was teasing Tarzan. And in that he was terrific.

There were lots of games that Roger and I played with Tarzan. One was to sneak up and hit him and then run out of his reach and make him keep chasing us to get us back. That one was almost like tag. And it was also fun to hide in a tree and see if we could hit him with mango pits. But the best was when Roger and I would rush him when he had just found a nice mango or orange and was about to eat it. One of us would grab it from him and toss it to the other. Then we'd both run and toss it back and forth while Tarzan screeched and screamed and ran back and forth between us trying to get it back. It was just like a game I used to play in the park, called Monkey in the Middle, only this was even better.

"Hey, Insect!" I signed as Tarzan made a desperate lunge for his fruit. "Why don't you *fly* up to catch it!" And then I'd nearly fall down from laughing so hard. It kept up like that until either Tarzan finally managed to grab it back from us or it got so bruised and squishy that nobody wanted it. Then Tarzan would find himself another fruit; and if he didn't run away fast enough with it, the whole game would start over again.

When he had enough, Tarzan ran away to a safe

distance from us and then just stood there, screaming at us and even making his strange finger-jabbing sign in the air, as if he thought he were telling us just what he thought of us. For some reason, making his sign seemed to frustrate him even more. After a moment or two of that, he'd bang the ground, make his sign again, and usually end up screaming till he was hoarse. I laughed so hard I could hardly stand up.

Sometimes I'd see Nibbles watching us from a distance, with a concerned look on her face, and I'd feel a little funny about what we were doing. But, as Roger said, he was just a dummy, so it really didn't make any difference, anyway. And besides, the games were just too funny.

But one afternoon Tarzan did something that stopped our laughing.

We were walking toward the beach when we saw him crouched in front of a tiny hill just outside the forest. At first I didn't know what he was doing. As I got closer, I could see his movements more clearly. He was holding a small stick and pushing it into a hole on top of the hill. The hill was evidently a termite nest, because when he pulled the stick out again, a horde of little white bugs was clinging onto it. In a flash, Tarzan clamped his teeth down onto the stick and swallowed the termites. Then he repeated the process.

"Hey, look!" I laughed. "The insect's eating insects!"

I nudged Roger. But the laugh stuck in my throat. A strange feeling was growing in my stomach, a feeling like . . . hunger. And Nibbles and Roger seemed to be feeling the same thing; we watched in fascination. Back home, I would have found the very idea disgusting. I wondered why I didn't now. All I knew was that each little termite suddenly seemed like a morsel of meat. And that meat, any kind of meat, was what I needed. One by one we sat down and watched, our mouths watering.

Tarzan barely glanced up at us; he just kept fishing for termites and swallowing them down. Before long we could see the whole procedure. When one stick got bent, Tarzan interrupted himself to go find another and strip off the leaves; then he'd start over again. Sometimes he prepared a few stick at a time and laid them in a row beside the termite nest; other times he found and worked with one stick at a time. At last he seemed to have eaten his fill, and he knuckle-walked off into the forest.

"I've heard of this," Roger signed half to himself, "but I never saw it before. He may have learned it as a youngster in the wild, before he was captured."

We approached the termite nest and tried Tarzan's technique, first Roger, then me, and finally Nibbles. It was harder than it looked. It took practice to find and prepare the right kind of stick and especially to bite down on the termites and swallow them before *they* could bite us—as Nibbles painfully found out. But I learned how to do it. The termites were crunchy—a little like raw peas in a pod, but squirmier. And they were what I needed. Courtesy of Tarzan.

Roger looked down at the pile of used sticks and pursed his lips. "He's undoubtedly a primitive chimp," he signed. "But he may, after all, be teachable."

He gazed out toward where Tarzan had disappeared into the forest and frowned, deep in thought.

❧ 10 ❧
Something
Spectacular

My opinion of Tarzan rose a little bit after that, but not a *whole* lot. He'd picked up one survival skill somewhere, and I was glad he had; but he still seemed crazy in most other ways.

But Roger's change of attitude was amazing, as abrupt as anything I'd ever seen. Not only were there no more games of tag or Monkey in the Middle. *Now* Roger seemed positively *friendly*. Whenever he saw Tarzan, he'd approach with a grunt of greeting and an exaggerated sign for "Hello." He'd grin and bob his head, even try to pat Tarzan reassuringly when he could get close enough (which wasn't often). But Tarzan had good reason not to trust Roger, and he continued to keep his distance and have as little as possible to do with us.

In the meantime, we'd begun to find birds' eggs, which we ate raw, of course. We just popped them whole into our mouths, shell and all, and bit down, making something like a crunchy milkshake (my own discovery). Between the eggs and the termites and the fruits and vegetables, we were now eating pretty well, and we had time to begin to think about other things. Roger even began some kind of building project: he experimented with tying thick branches together with vines to make some kind of a squarish frame; but he never answered us when we asked what he was doing.

My dreams began to be different, too. One night, I even dreamed I was back home in the living room, sitting in front of the TV set. When I turned it on, I saw myself climbing and swinging through the trees, just like Jungle Man; then I saw myself jump down, and the screen went to a close-up. I made a funny face, and then everyone was laughing and applauding—and it almost hurt, how badly I wanted it. I'd almost forgotten.

It wasn't just being on TV. To me, TV had been

everything. My favorite show back home had been *Jungle Man*. I'd watched him every day. And Jungle Man could do *anything*. He could climb trees, jump off a cliff, swing from vines—nothing could stop him, no bad guy was too mean for him, nothing was too big for him to handle. And even if he got flattened like a pancake, a minute later he was fine again. He was the strongest, smartest, toughest guy there was. I wanted to be just like him.

That probably would have been all there was to it—I mean, just watching other people on TV. But then one day, a long time ago, some people had come to see me in the apartment and they'd pointed some bright lights at me. At first I hadn't wanted to play— the lights hurt my eyes and made me blink, and the people didn't even have anything good for me to eat, so I'd just kept running away from them and going back into my room. But Dr. Franklin had made me come out again and show them all my signs, and I've always liked having an audience. Pretty soon I was showing them some of my tricks, too—like flipping around on the couch and jumping from the dresser, and even a few things I just thought up on the spur of the moment, like making funny faces at them. A few days later, I was watching *The Six O'Clock News* show—I'd never liked the news very much, but tonight Dr. Franklin had made me watch it—and all of a sudden, *I* was on TV: There I was, doing all the things I'd shown them! I couldn't believe it. "That's

Danny, that's Danny!" I'd signed over and over. I was so excited I was jumping up and down in front of the set, and everyone in the apartment was laughing and cheering and patting me on the back—and suddenly it had seemed that *I was* just like Jungle Man. He wasn't just someone on TV anymore. *I* could be on TV too! And at that moment, I'd known what I wanted, and what I'd always want.

And now, after all this time on the island, suddenly I was dreaming and thinking about it again, with a pang that surprised me. Strange that I should suddenly want that again now, and so badly, when I wasn't even off the island yet. I guess it came of having the time to think about it. I gritted my teeth and put it out of my mind again.

There was time for lots of things now. Time for play, time for squabbling a little, time for resting in the sun. But most of all, there was time to think about civilization. And a plan to get back there.

There was a lot we missed: the familiar foods and surroundings, the variety of activities. And people. Especially people—not just our special friends, like Peggy or Nibbles's Dr. Denton—but people in general. Frankly, I missed the attention. And, now that I had the time to think about it, I was lonely.

"We need a plan," I signed one morning.

"You said that once before," Roger replied.

"I did?"

"A long time ago." He scratched his chin. "Yes, you're quite right. I think we can assume that Dr. Simeon and Brian *will* eventually return to check on us, just as they said they would, and it could be any day now. Clearly, we can't afford to be unprepared when they come."

Nibbles watched him closely. "A plan to get back home again?"

"Yes. A plan to get home." Roger frowned in concentration. "As I see it, we have two choices. One is, we can make another attempt to show them how miserably we're doing here. Unfortunately, they're bound to be skeptical after the last time, and the very fact that we've survived this long argues against that." He paused. "Our other choice is a more honorable one: to do something so spectacular that the humans will *want* us back and will wonder how they ever could have done without us, something so spectacular that they'll even be willing to take us back on our *own* terms."

"And *you* said *that* before," I signed. "We got *that* far our first day here."

"Or some of us did," Roger signed mildly. "But while you and Nibbles were busy tickling each other, *I've* been giving quite a bit of thought to the idea. And I just may have a solution."

Roger sat down and paused for a moment. He had our attention.

"It's tricky," he continued. "Not only do we have to *do* something spectacular, we have to make sure they *realize* we're doing something spectacular. And that's not as easy as it sounds. Just think about it—" He scratched a toenail. "Think what they saw the last time around: They saw us sign, on numerous occasions. They interacted with us themselves; they had entire conversations with us, on the very spot where we're sitting now. But somehow it never clicked with them that they were seeing something extraordinary, something that would justify continuing the experiment. Why?" Roger looked from me to Nibbles and back again. "Why? Because so far all they could report on was their own subjective experience!"

"Huh?"

Roger licked his fingers. "Let me put it this way. As of their last visit, Dr. Simeon and Brian could go back to the other scientists and the people who give the money out, and they could say, 'Gee, guys, it sure *seems* like the chimps are really talking to us!' And the scientists would say, 'Really?' And Dr. Simeon could say, 'Really! This isn't like any trained dog act. This time they're really talking, I swear it!' And then the scientists would say, 'No kidding! Well, gee, this is all really interesting, but isn't that the same thing you said when you had the chimps back in the lab? Sure, it *seems* like they're talking— but can you *prove* it?' "

114

"You mean they need evidence."

"Right!" Roger pounded his fist on the ground. "Hard, scientific evidence! The kind they get in a language lab."

I groaned.

"I know," Roger signed. "And most ways of doing it, we'd just end up in the same dumb labs again, with the same dumb humans, which none of us wants."

Nibbles spoke up for the first time. "*I* want it," she signed.

Roger shrugged. "Which *most* of us don't want," he corrected himself. "I believe Danny, for one, had some plans about a film career. And of course, I had some plans, too."

A film career. All at once my dreams flooded through again. I struggled to follow his line of thought.

"So we need evidence," I signed. "Or *they* need evidence; but we have to help them get it 'cause they're too dumb to do it by themselves. And even then, the best we can hope for is to be sent back to a lab. No film career for me, no language research career for you."

"Unless . . ." Roger scratched his nose. "Unless . . ."

I nearly screamed in exasperation. "Unless *what?*"

Roger smiled. "Supposing we were to set up our *own* language lab—right here on the island?"

I stared at him blankly.

"That's right, Danny!" Roger gave a high-spirited hoot. "*Give* them their evidence—our *own* way! They like labs? *Give* them a lab—but not like any they've ever seen before! Can you imagine their reaction? They leave us on this island, hoping we'll just survive, they come back and find *chimps being taught language—not by humans, but by other chimps!* Can you believe it? It's perfect!"

"What's so perfect about it?"

"Don't you see?" Roger rose to his feet. "If we did that, they could never explain it all away as 'just subjective impressions.' Our language lab would be a *fact*! They'd never let a chance like that get away! They'd take us back to civilization—all together! We'd have a regular house, with our own quarters, our own schoolroom, regular meals! Instead of participating in demeaning experiments for humans, we could run our own schools, our own way, for ourselves—with dignity! Think of the publicity! Danny, you could be a media star in no time! Nibbles, you could visit your daddy whenever you wanted; he might even come there to live with us!"

My heart beat faster. I felt myself getting carried along with Roger's vision. Nibbles's eyes glistened. There was also a glint in the corner of Roger's eye, something I didn't quite trust. I pulled myself back.

"That's wonderful." I paused a moment, thinking hard. "And just incidentally, you get a start on your career as a humble language researcher."

Roger looked down in apparent embarrassment. "You're quite right. I guess I did get carried away a bit. We'll leave visions of the future for later. Right now our job is to set up a simple lab for the three of us right here."

Nibbles sat up. "Will they really let Daddy live with us?"

"I'm sure they will," signed Roger.

"And Mommy? And Kathy? And kitty?"

Roger nodded. He'd tell her anything. And she'd believe it.

Nibbles smiled. "Then let's make the lab now, like you said!" A puzzled look crossed her face. "But who will teach us in the lab?"

"He thought you'd never ask."

Roger ignored me. "Well . . ." He frowned. "We must choose carefully. We need a chimp who is more verbal than the others, perhaps more intelligent, one who has studied the scientists and knows their language-lab techniques. . . ."

Nibbles brightened. "It's you!"

Roger looked surprised. "Well, no, I really don't know if—"

"It's you, it's you!" Nibbles jumped up and down. "It has to be!"

"Well, perhaps you're right." Roger looked at me.

117

"You understand, Danny, this really is necessary. And it's only a temporary measure. Once they take us back to civilization—"

"—they'll remember that you were the one who was teaching, and you'll *still* be in charge."

"I'm sorry you feel that way, Danny." Roger stroked his chin. "Listen, how would it be if some of the time I taught you, and some of the time you could help me teach?"

"Help you teach who?"

"Well, Tarzan, if we can catch him. He knows even less language than you do." He caught my look. "A *lot* less," he added quickly. "If we can teach someone like him, it will *really* be convincing. It might even be the clincher."

"Thanks." I chewed on a leaf. "And how do you think you'll get *him* to go along with it?"

Roger gave me a mild look. "Oh, I think I can persuade him. And if worse comes to worst, there are always other means." He let his gaze wander for an instant along the beach toward the frame he was constructing, then quickly looked back to me again. And suddenly I understood, understood what Roger had been so busy with, the past few days. And it almost took my breath away.

"It's a cage," I signed at last. "You're building a cage for Tarzan."

His eyes shifted uneasily; then he yawned. "Well, at least a poor attempt at one—and only as a last resort." His eyes scanned Nibbles and me. "It's standard lab technique, really. See, that gives us control over his food supply, so then he has no choice: no talkee, no foodee."

Nibbles's mouth dropped, and mine did, too; it seemed as if we were seeing Roger for the first time. I didn't have any great liking for Tarzan, and I'd undeniably had my share of fun at his expense. But just the same, a *cage!* It was bad enough when *humans* did these things to us. The idea of one chimp doing it to another made me sick.

Roger saw his mistake. "Well, it was just a thought."

"Sure," I signed. "And if he's a slow learner, we can rig up a device for electric shocks!"

"Now, nobody said anything about electric shocks." Roger looked from Nibbles to me. "I wasn't aware that Tarzan was such a great friend of yours."

I stood up. "Is that what's waiting for *us* when you set up your wonderful chimp-run language lab back in civilization: cages and controlled food supplies?"

"No, of course not!" He paced back and forth. "We were talking about Tarzan, remember? A primitive, unpredictable chimp, out here in the wild with very little other means of control available. I suggested the cage as a last resort, if all else fails. It was just an idea off the top of my head, and I see now it was a bad one. I'm sorry I had the poor taste to mention it." He sat down and gave us a pained look, his eyes wide. "Danny, Nibbles, could you really think that I'd plan a cage for *you*?"

He kept looking at us, but we didn't sign anything. Then he turned away. He sat like that a long time, staring into the distance.

I looked at his face. I wasn't sure I trusted him, but perhaps I'd been too hard on him. He looked back to us.

"No," I signed, "I don't think you want to put us in cages."

"Thank you." Roger sat up again. "Look, we'll forget about Tarzan. We'll run a language lab just for the three of us. Out in the open: no cages, no desks. Just the three of us. We'll show the humans what chimps can do!"

I looked him straight in the eye. "I don't want to be in your language lab."

"It's better than being in a lab run by humans!"

"I'm not so sure I see the difference."

Roger stood up. "Okay." He nodded. "All right. Fine. Then I guess that leaves us with our last alternative: just stay and find a way to make a life for ourselves here, on this island." He smiled faintly. "With the cannibals."

A chill ran up and down my spine. Nibbles shrank back.

"You know, I didn't want to alarm you," Roger continued, "but I saw something yesterday when I was gathering breakfast. Something rather . . . disturbing."

Nibbles drew her lips back into a frightened grimace. "What did you see?"

"More footprints, for one thing, like the ones we saw the first day. On *our* side of the foliage barrier."

"You mean they're—"

"Exploring, probably, just as we were. It means we can't count on their staying on their side of the island forever. One group must have just gone by a short time before I got there. I think I even heard them—hooting, screaming, and crashing around. They sounded very fierce and dangerous."

Nibbles looked at her hands and breathed quickly.

I looked at Roger. "Aah, you're just trying to scare us."

"I didn't invent these footprints, Danny. You saw them just as close as I did."

Nibbles glanced toward the other side of the island. "Maybe—maybe we should do what Roger says."

"I don't think so!" I pounded my chest.

"But if there are cannibals. . . !"

"No!" I didn't really have an answer for that one, so I just repeated myself. "No!"

"But why not?" Nibbles was almost crying.

"Because I don't trust him, that's why not! Don't you see what he's doing? *He* gets a tremendous start on *his* career—we even help him to do it—and *we* get nothing! All we get is to be subjects in his language lab! And who knows *what* happens to us then?"

"But he said—"

"Yeah." I pursed my lips at Roger. "*He* said. *After* he gets his language lab, *then* maybe somehow I'll get to be a star and you'll get to see your daddy."

"Right, that's what he said!"

"Right. *If* you can believe him!"

Roger stepped right up to me and glared into my eyes. There was hardly any space between us.

"Danny, I'm trying to be patient with you," he signed.

"Why?" I glared right back at him. "You going to do something to me?"

We stared at each other for what seemed like hours. It was finally Roger who made a move.

"All right," Roger signed at last, still glaring at me. "All right. But remember, Danny: *I gave you a chance.*"

I bared my teeth. "What's *that* supposed to mean?"

"Nothing." Roger broke the gaze. "Nothing at all." He turned and walked a short distance away, then sat down and wrinkled his brow. He looked into the distance.

And that was when we heard the rumbling.

❧ 11 ❧
I Take the Lead

The threat hung heavy in the air. A chance? What chance?

I felt a rumbling in my chest, a trembling of anger and excitement. *Roger* had given *me* a chance? Or else *what*?

I glared at him, but he didn't return my gaze. Instead he was looking up, up into the sky, and so was Nibbles.

And suddenly, I realized that the rumbling in my chest wasn't only from excitement. It was from a sound high above us, coming closer and closer. A sound I should have recognized.

It was from the airplane.

I stared at it stupidly for what seemed like a long time, then started to break for the beach.

"Wait!" Roger gave a quick, jerky motion to catch my eye. "They're not landing on the beach. They're landing on the mainland."

He was right. I stopped myself, feeling foolish.

The plane roared overhead and lowered toward the mainland. I covered my ears, but Roger never flinched.

"They'll probably have to set up camp when they get there," Roger signed. "That gives us at most until tomorrow morning to do something, if we're *ever* to get home again. Do you understand me, Danny? *Home.* To sleep in your own bed, in your own room, to eat regular food, to see your friends again. *A chance to be a star, Danny. . . .*" I shook my head violently, trying to shut out the words, but Roger kept going. "It's our only chance, Danny. We need a plan, and we need it *now*. And it so happens, I've got the only plan going."

I shook my head, once, twice, again and again. Part of me wanted to say, Yes, we'll do it, *anything,* quick before they leave us, just get us home again! But I couldn't—not the way Roger wanted. It wasn't just that it was unfair and Roger would be the boss. I could take that, if it would get us home. But Roger could be setting himself up as boss for *life,* and in a new lab that might be nothing *like* home. And more,

I just didn't trust him. I didn't have any other ideas, but I didn't trust Roger.

"Please!" Nibbles bobbed her head and crouched, doing everything she could to persuade me. Her eyes were wide with desperation. "Please Danny!"

"Danny!" Roger drew himself up to his full height. "You listen to me, and listen well." He glared. "I know that you've resented me. You've disliked my bossing, my deciding what has to be done, my goading you when you would rather not have been bothered. But the fact is, Danny, that *you and Nibbles are alive today because of one reason: and that reason is me.*" He looked us full in the face, daring us to deny it. And, as much as it rankled me, I couldn't.

"*I* pulled at you," he continued. "*I* coaxed you. *I* needled you. I spent my own energies to keep *you* going at times when you were both ready to give up and die. Why?" His eyes drilled into us. "*Because I knew that this moment would come. And I wanted to be prepared.*" He looked from me to Nibbles and back again. "Danny, Nibbles, you were saved for a purpose. Yes, we want to get home. We *all* do, and we *will*. But there's more than that, much more." He swallowed. "Danny, Nibbles. We have the opportunity to do an incredible thing here: to turn around the relationship between chimps and humans once and for all, to finally put ourselves on an equal footing, to manage our own affairs as equals among the humans. An *incredible* thing, a thing that has never before been done in the history of the world. But we can do this only if we all work together to put this over. The humans are here, they're back, there's no time for squabbling among ourselves. Now is our only chance.

"It's up to you, Danny; the choice is yours."

I felt that old tingling feeling that Roger could start in me with his words. But I fought it down.

"It all sounds beautiful, Roger. It really does." I looked straight into his eyes. "But we'd still be working on what *you* want. And *you'd* still be the boss."

Roger looked back at me. He paused. "Then it's no?"

"It's no."

His nostrils flared. "Danny, you leave me very little choice." He signed with quick, tight movements, practically slamming one hand into the other. "Very little choice at all."

He broke away and walked down the beach, breathing heavily, showing more feeling than I'd ever before seen in him. Then he seemed to control himself; he took a deep breath and walked back in the other direction, rubbing his chin thoughtfully, his brows knitted. It was a long time before he looked at me again. Then he sighed.

"Maybe you're right," he signed at last. "Maybe I'm being selfish. I was trying to find a way to get us all out of here, so naturally my mind went to ideas that I'm familiar with. And sometimes my ideas *can* be rather grand." He cocked his head in a gesture of self-mockery. "But perhaps it wasn't right to choose a way that would be most helpful to only one of us."

I watched him closely. "That's for sure."

"Maybe there's some other way to get us home. Perhaps, for instance, some way to make use of your theatrical gifts, Danny, and make Dr. Simeon aware of the financial potential in that area."

"Yes?" I searched his face, feeling a strange combination of hope and distrust; but his expression gave me no clue.

Roger appeared not to see me; he seemed deep in thought. "Yes," he continued, "we could—" He stopped. "Oh, but what am I thinking? That would present the same problem as my first plan."

"What's that?"

"Why, being most helpful to only one of us. I'm sure you'd never go along with it." I saw that glint in his eye again, but I had to know what he was saying.

"Never go along with *what*?" I signed.

But Roger wasn't looking. "It's a pity," he continued, as if to himself. "We've even got a staging area right here on the island, just going to waste. It's a shame. . . ."

The thought dawned on me. "You mean . . . you mean we could put on a play for them, right there at the staging area!"

"It's a thought," signed Roger. "We'd need a star, of course. And I'm simply not up to that kind of theatrics myself. But perhaps another chimp . . ."

"You mean me." I thought it out carefully, trying not to get carried away. "I could be the star."

"Why, yes!" signed Roger. "That's an idea!"

"And . . . you wouldn't mind that?"

Roger's face softened. "As long as it gets us home. That *is* the main idea, isn't it?"

My mouth opened, and for just a moment I thought I'd cry. Roger saw the expression on my face.

"I know what it means to you, Danny. Don't you think I know? And, if we can use your gifts to help all of us—well, I won't stand in your way."

I thought of how I'd been acting, and how Roger had kept us going, and suddenly I felt ashamed. I had to trust him then, at least about the play. I felt I just had to.

"I'll do the best acting job ever!" I signed. "I'll do it for all of us!"

"I know you will." He patted me on the shoulder. "And then, when they see the talent you've got, and they realize how you're being wasted on this island—"

"—then they'll know where I *really* belong; and they'll take me to Hollywood! And then in a little while, I'll be a star, and I could tell them to take you and Nibbles back, too!"

"Why, that's wonderful!" signed Roger. "Only do you think you could make that last part right away, instead of 'in a little while'?"

"Well . . ." I paused uncomfortably. "Roger, these things take time. They won't really listen to me until I'm a star, and I don't expect to become a star overnight. It might take days and days."

"*Days and days?*" Nibbles' eyes widened. "You mean, we'll just have to *wait* here with the *cannibals?*"

I'd almost forgotten about the cannibals, and I didn't like seeing Nibbles look like that. I thought a moment. "I've got it: when they decide to take me back, I'll just tell them my friends come with me. If *they* don't go, *I* don't go! If I put it that way, they'll *have* to take you. They won't have any choice!"

Roger gave me a benevolent look. "Danny, you're a good chimp." He placed a hand on my shoulder. "Now, we'll need some kind of a play, some kind of a story. I think I may have some ideas along those lines. And we'll also need a director."

"You mean the guy who tells everyone what to do?"

"Well, more or less, yes. I think I may have some talents in that area."

So Roger would still be the boss. But I guessed maybe that wouldn't be so terrible. I nodded.

"Good!" Roger smiled again. "Now there's one thing I must ask of you: nobody tell Brian or Dr. Simeon about the play."

"Why not?"

His eyes glinted. "I think it will be most effective if we surprise them. Let it dawn on them gradually that what they're seeing is a theatrical production. At all costs, they mustn't know that they're to witness a play."

I looked doubtful. "But what if they don't understand?"

"That will be up to you, Danny, by the strength of your performance—to *make* them understand! The shock of recognition should be tremendous!"

I thought a minute. "Do you really think so?"

"Believe me, Danny"— Roger patted me encouragingly— "the added realism will give your performance a power you can't imagine!"

I nodded. Keeping a secret was hard; but, after all, they were letting me be the star. It seemed a small price to pay.

✶ 12 ✶
Total Theater

It's a good thing we had the play to work on. Otherwise I don't know how we could have stood it to wait for Dr. Simeon and Brian. But the play kept us busy.

We spent most of the day at the staging area, rehearsing our parts. There wasn't a set script, so we had to improvise a lot. Roger would give us a few key lines and the general story, and we had to make up the rest. Nibbles had a lot of trouble getting the hang of it. Mostly she just signed "Yes" or "No" or "Okay." But I was really hot: lines just kept coming to me, faster than I could even sign them.

The story was Roger's idea. We decided it would

be most effective if we did something relevant to our own situation: what Roger called "making a statement." So our play was the story of three brave, desperate chimps who are surprised and driven from their homes by evil robbers. The chimps band together and fight—until finally, through a mixture of cunning and courage, they capture the robbers and get their old homes back. Somehow, every time we rehearsed it, it came out different. Unless you knew the story already, you couldn't always even figure out what was happening. Just about the only thing that came out exactly the same each time was my swinging from a vine and leaping onto the chief robber; then I tied him up with strong vines and signed, "This I do for all chimps everywhere! Freedom for chimps!" It was the one line Roger insisted on, and it was actually my favorite part in the whole play.

"I don't know," Roger signed after a worried spell of pacing and rubbing his chin. "Something is still missing."

"Like what?"

"Like the robbers."

"But we've been through that," I signed. "*We* have to play the three chimps. And we get all confused when any of us doubles as a robber. So all we can do is just pretend that the robbers are there and explain it to the audience!"

"It's not very convincing." Roger frowned. "And not very professional."

"Well?"

Roger knitted his brows. "Why not let Brian and Dr. Simeon be the robbers?"

"But they're the audience!"

"Exactly!" Roger slapped his hand to his thigh. "Audience involvement! It's the latest thing!"

Huh?"

"It's called total theater. Don't you see? We do away with the distinction between the audience and the play—the audience *is* the play! Total involvement—total theater!"

"You mean they watch and act at the same time?"

"Exactly!"

I thought a minute. "It's interesting. But doesn't that mean we have to warn them, so we can all rehearse?"

"No!" Roger threw his hands in all directions. "Definitely not! The whole point of total theater is to make the theatrical experience part of real life—and life just happens! Did anybody warn you before you were born? No! Did they warn you when they shot you full of sedatives and stuck you in a box and shipped you off to Chimp Island? Again, no!"

I flushed with anger, remembering. "You're right!"

"Of course I'm right! Through this play, we'll

133

share our experience with them. Let them know what it means to be a chimp!"

I felt that stirring in my chest again, and this time I didn't fight it down. I couldn't have said no if I'd tried.

We woke next morning to a distant rumbly sound we all recognized: the motorboat! They were here; they were really back for us! My stomach went all jittery. I thought of our play again and made sure I hadn't forgotten my part. This was it!

We hurried to the beach and came to a tearing stop, just as Brian and Dr. Simeon climbed out of the boat.

"Hello!" signed Dr. Simeon and tripped over a small rock.

"Hello," we signed back. We stood waiting as they walked toward us.

"How are you?"

I was too excited to answer. I just jumped up and down, hoo-ing.

Dr. Simeon smiled. "How are you?" he repeated, making his signs even bigger.

"Fine!" I signed.

He grinned broadly. "You *look* very well. You all look wonderful!" His signs were so big, he almost looked like Roger talking to Tarzan.

Nibbles stepped forward. "Did you see Daddy? When you went back home, did you see my daddy?"

"Well, no, we didn't actually see him . . ."

"Oh." Nibbles' face fell.

"Dr. Simeon and Brian," Roger broke in. "We have something to show you—something *very* important."

"Yes?"

"If you'll follow us a short distance . . ."

"Well, I suppose we could; we just wanted to look around a little first and see what's been happening, but—"

"It really is important," signed Roger. "It's something we've been working on."

"Really?" Dr. Simeon raised his eyebrows in interest. We had him! "Well, in that case, certainly, we'll—"

"Hoo-*hoo!*" said Tarzan, running from the other end of the beach. "Hoo-hoo-*hoo!*"

Before anyone could move, he had barreled almost into Dr. Simeon and grabbed him by his pant leg.

"Well, hello, Tarzan!" signed Dr. Simeon, hopping to regain his balance. "We're glad to see you, too. We—"

"Hoo-hoo-*hoo!*" Tarzan yanked again, almost ripping the fabric. Dr. Simeon stumbled another step forward, and Tarzan pulled again.

"Yes, I *said*, hello! Hello!"

Tarzan gave another yank—and pulled Dr. Simeon with him.

"Now, Tarzan, this is enough, really it is!" whined the scientist as he made his way unwillingly across the beach. Brian smirked behind his hand. "Stop it, Tarzan, stop—oop!—please stop it!" Tarzan just kept pulling, not frantically, but with determination. "I really don't see what—"

With a sudden jolt, Tarzan stopped and released his grip, then pointed to a spot on the sand. Dr. Simeon staggered one more step forward before stopping and looking where Tarzan had pointed. The rest of us looked, too.

In the sand, Tarzan had drawn a large circle. Inside the circle, at the top, was a medium-sized circle. Under the medium-sized circle were rows of tiny circles. And underneath it all was a straight line with four more circles. It looked something like this:

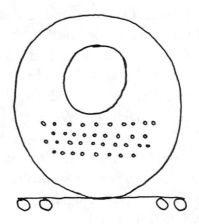

Then Tarzan started his strange finger-sign again —holding his hands out, palms down, at chest level, and jabbing downward with his fingers. Only this time, after a moment, he sat down in front of his drawing and put his fingers over the tiny circles, while he continued making the sign.

Dr. Simeon gave him a long, puzzled look. "Tarzan, Tarzan," he signed at last. "Why don't you just *sign* what you want?" He turned to go, and of course, Tarzan started screaming again and jumping up and down and pointing to his beautiful picture. Which, as far as I could see, meant absolutely nothing to anyone.

Brian strolled over for a better look. I caught a few of his words. "Tarzan," he said, "you're probably the only chimp here who hasn't been trying to put something over on us, and *you*'ve got to be the crazy one!" He looked down at Tarzan's drawing—and stopped short. An expression of shock came over his face. He looked up at Dr. Simeon, then down at the drawing again. Then he pulled Dr. Simeon off to the side, and they spoke in very low voices. They kept looking from Tarzan to his drawing and back to each other again, and I caught a few words like, "Do you really think. . . ?" and "But I was certain. . . !" Finally Dr. Simeon pulled a small clipboard out from his safari shirt and looked over some writing on it. He looked first at one page and then another. Then his face got panicky, and he kept flipping back and forth between the two pages. Finally he just stopped, put his hand to his cheek, and let out a groan. Brian rolled his eyes.

I didn't know exactly what was happening, but I

could tell that somehow Tarzan had suddenly become the center of attention. Today of all days! They might forget about us *entirely*, and we'd *never* get to do our play! I ran toward Brian and Dr. Simeon and starting signing and grunting for their attention. But they just ignored me! I couldn't believe it! Dr. Simeon raised a finger, signaling for Tarzan to wait for him; and Tarzan seemed to understand. Then Dr. Simeon and Brian headed for the boat. I ran after them, signing, "Wait! Wait!" But it was no use. They started the motor and speeded out toward the mainland.

We were all at the edge of the water now, watching after the boat. Tarzan was waiting impatiently, leaning forward, straining to see. Nibbles and I kept signing to each other, asking each other what was happening; but of course neither of us knew. Roger just shook his head and sat, watching calmly.

It seemed a very long time before I saw the boat coming back. They landed it near the rocks again and lifted out something in a cardboard crate. They carried this over to the beach and started unpacking it.

Tarzan watched bug-eyed. Before whatever it was was even out of the crate, he had recognized it. He leaped and gave a whoop, raced toward the machine, and flung his arms around it. His chest heaved in convulsive sobs; he hugged the machine and wouldn't let go. Brian and Dr. Simeon grinned at each other; they had to weave in and out among Tarzan's limbs to finish unpacking it.

"It" was a little red wagon, the kind you sometimes see kids playing with, with a machine bolted to it. The machine looked like a TV screen attached to an electric typewriter. When it was unpacked, Tarzan darted to the front, seated himself at the keyboard, and started typing as fast as he could. With each key he typed, a different shape flashed on the TV screen—shapes unlike any printing I'd ever seen.

My jaw hung open. Now I knew the meaning of Tarzan's strange, finger-jabbing sign. And I also knew where I'd seen him before.

Tarzan typed like a maniac—even faster than Dr. Franklin—as if he couldn't wait to let out everything he'd been unable to say for all the time he'd been on the island. From time to time he'd stop for a moment and let Dr. Simeon type something in reply; but he was so anxious he often broke back in before Dr. Simeon even seemed to be finished.

"What is it?" asked Nibbles.

"It's Yerkish," I signed.

"Yerkish?"

"It's a way of talking by computer." I swallowed. "I think he's the same chimp I saw on *Sixty Minutes*, the same time I was on." Back then, the computer had been a much bigger one, filling up nearly the entire room; but this seemed to be the same principle.

139

Nibbles looked puzzled. "A computer?"

"Don't you see? They taught *us* to speak by sign language. Well, they took some other chimps and taught *them* to speak by computer: they punch the keys, and the computer makes the sign."

Nibbles watched Tarzan a while longer. "You mean he's *not* crazy? And he's *not* a dummy?"

I shook my head. Nibbles grunted in understanding.

Tarzan typed some more and gave Dr. Simeon a hurt, soulful look.

"Yes, I know," Dr. Simeon said soothingly, as he typed in reply. "I know. *You* try tell us, and no we understand!"

Tarzan typed some more and gave the three of us an accusing look.

"Oh . . ." Dr. Simeon replied. "They be mean to you."

Tarzan nodded.

"Well—no you see them now. Now you come with us please. Okay?"

Dr. Simeon turned off the machine and took Tarzan by the hand. Tarzan walked with him, pulling his little red wagon behind him. Brian and Dr. Simeon lifted the wagon and machine back into the boat. Then they all climbed in, and Brian prepared to start the motor.

Tarzan looked steadily at the three of us, then raised his thumb to his nose while twiddling his four other fingers and blew us a raspberry. It wasn't exactly American Sign Language, but he got his message across. Then the boat started.

I just watched, stunned, as the boat puttered off. But it didn't go out toward the mainland; this time it only went out a short distance and then turned to run in the same direction as the shore, until it disappeared behind the cove.

I was still watching when I realized that Roger had been busy for some time, kicking up the sand over Tarzan's footprints. Something about his movement seemed false—apparently casual, but hurried at the same time. I rushed over; Roger saw me coming and gave one final kick.

"Imagine that!" he signed, and tried to make me follow in the other direction. "We really must talk!" He started signing a mile a minute, pulling me off toward the jungle. I resisted.

"What were *you* doing?" I signed.

"Why—" He looked at me. "Whatever do you mean?"

I searched the ground, but I was too late: the footprints were covered. I gave Roger a hard stare; he just looked back innocently and then strolled a little farther along the beach, kicking the sand before him.

I didn't know why Roger didn't want me to see those footprints. But whatever information they contained was lost now forever.

❦ 13 ❦
Freedom for Chimps!

It was some time now since Brian and Dr. Simeon had left. The sun was already high in the sky, and still there was no sign of them. My stomach rumbled, but somehow I didn't feel like eating.

"What do we do now?" Nibbles asked me.

I shook my head.

"Where did they take Tarzan?"

I couldn't answer that one, either.

Roger turned toward us on the beach. " 'What do we do now?' We wait till they come back, and then we do exactly what we had planned to do: our play."

"If they even remember that we exist by now." I spat.

"And what does that mean?"

"*You* know."

"I *don't* know."

"Our whole ideas was to show them that *we're* something special, that we're worth having back in civilization. What can we possibly show them after Tarzan?" I flung myself on the ground.

Roger frowned sternly. "Danny, I'm surprised at you!"

"Why? *We* can't run a computer! We can't even type! We . . . we can't even *read!*"

Nibbles stifled a sob. She evidently saw my point.

"So?" Roger stomped the ground. "*And Tarzan can't speak sign language!*"

"That's diff—"

"It's not different! He was as helpless without his computer as we would be *with* it! Without his computer, that chimp is nothing; at least *we* always have our hands!"

I thought a minute, starting to feel a little better.

"He was taught to speak one way, we were taught to speak another, that's all," Roger continued. "The display on the TV screen may look pretty impressive; but every time he presses a key, he's only doing what he was taught to do. But our play, on the other hand —no one taught us how to put on a play. Tarzan may know how to do what he was taught. But we know how to go *beyond* what we were taught!"

I sat up. "Do you really think they'll see it that way?"

"Unless they're even stupider than we've thought."

I nodded. Roger made sense. So all there was to do now was wait; that was the hard part.

The shadows were getting long when we heard the motorboat again. I was on my feet in no time, straining to catch sight of it. Then it rounded the cove and headed toward the beach. So at least they had come back; it was all I could do to keep from crying with relief. Then Dr. Simeon and Brian stepped out.

They looked sweaty, and Dr. Simeon wasn't wearing his phony-excited smile anymore. I wondered if he only put it on in the mornings. Just from the way they moved, I could tell they were tired from something. *Really* tired. I felt a sinking feeling in my stomach, and then a growing anger. They leave us alone for days and days, and then come back *like this*? On our one chance to get off this island? What kind of audience would they make now?

"Hello," signed Dr. Simeon. The sign was a little sloppy, without his usual energy. "We're sorry we took so long. You see, we had to take Tarzan somewhere else and then help him get settled."

"Where?" I signed. "Where is Tarzan?"

"Well, he was never supposed to be here with you.

144

It was a mistake. So we took him where he was supposed to be."

Which of course didn't answer my question. But at least he admitted he had made a mistake. Dr. Franklin never did that.

"Did you practice your climbing? Are you getting your food okay now?"

"We are learning," signed Roger. "We still need much practice."

Dr. Simeon nodded. "You look as if you're eating well. You can show us what you're doing tomorrow." He looked at his watch. "I'm afraid we won't have time to do very much today."

No time? My hands could hardly make the signs. "But . . ." I fumbled. "But—"

"Dr. Simeon," Roger interrupted, "and Brian. We have something to show you."

"Oh. Right." Dr. Simeon looked at us. "Well? what is it?"

"It's not here. You have to follow us."

"Where?"

"That way." Roger pointed along the path.

Dr. Simeon's eyes followed the path along into the distance. "Tomorrow," he signed. "Tomorrow, early in the morning."

I grunted, hitting my leg in frustration.

"No," signed Roger. "It must be now. It might not be there in the morning."

"What is it?"

"We can only show you."

Brian and Dr. Simeon exchanged glances. Brian muttered something I didn't quite catch; whatever it was, it didn't sound friendly.

"It's important," I signed. "It really is. And I can't wait!—I mean, it can't wait!"

"Tomorrow you'll wish you had seen it," signed Roger. "It could mean quite a bit for your studies."

Dr. Simeon eyed him closely. "What do you mean, about my studies?"

Roger just watched him. Dr. Simeon looked back to Brian again. "All right," he signed at last. "One quick look."

"Follow me!" Roger started down the path.

We walked a few minutes. In the time I'd been on the island, I had almost gotten used to the tall grasses and thorns along the path; but Brian and Dr. Simeon kept stopping to disentangle themselves and rub their skin where the thorns and grasses had scratched it.

Brian sucked at a scratch on his finger. "Just where exactly are we going?"

"Not far!" signed Roger.

He was telling the truth. The staging area was just ahead now. I could feel my heart beating faster, and my breaths getting short. I repeated my lines to myself to be sure I'd remember them and tried to imagine Brian and Dr. Simeon's reaction. They'd like it—they'd *have* to like it. And maybe—maybe, if they were *really* impressed—

I lurched forward and nearly went flying over the root I had tripped on. I regained my balance and pulled my mind back to where I was. Nibbles and I were in the lead now. I looked over my shoulder to see Brian and Roger walking together and Dr. Simeon in the rear. Strange. ". . . worried about Danny," Roger was signing. He saw me watching and stopped short.

"What's that supposed to mean?" I snorted.

"What?"

"Who's worried about me?"

Roger seemed to fumble for a moment. "Why . . . Why, you nearly landed on your face there. Why shouldn't I be worried?"

Somehow it still didn't sound right. I looked at him uncertainly.

"Really, now!" He caught up to me and patted my shoulder. "We can't have our star breaking his leg on us! Are you ready?"

I nodded. There wasn't time to try to figure out Roger. All I could worry about was our play.

"Roger! Danny!" Dr. Simeon called. We looked back toward him. "Stop!" he signed and caught up to us as we rounded a bend. "I think this is far enough for today, really. We're very tired, and we don't want to go any further!"

"Down there!" Roger pointed. Just beyond the

bend, at the bottom of three hills, was the staging area. "Very close, and it's all downhill."

"And all uphill on the way back," muttered Brian.

"You've already come this far," signed Roger.

Dr. Simeon hesitated. "Is it really, really important?"

"Yes," Roger and I signed almost in unison. "It really, really is."

"All right."

Nibbles, Roger, and I scrambled easily down the hill. Brian and Dr. Simeon took much longer, struggling over the rocks.

"I don't think they have much patience right now," Roger signed, "so maybe we'd better get right to the heart of it."

"You mean, when I jump down?"

"Right, your big scene. Once we grab them with that, we can always go back to the earlier parts."

I nodded.

"You keep a lookout," Roger continued, "and when you see me sign 'breakthrough,' you go on. That's your cue."

" 'Breakthrough.' Right."

"Places!" signed Roger.

I climbed up to a ledge above the cave and hid behind a large rock. My vines were there, right where I had left them, and so was one end of a thick, long vine that hung from a tree in front of the cave. I tugged at the long vine to test it; it was still strong.

"Places!" Roger signed again. Nibbles scurried inside the cave.

I heard Dr. Simeon and Brian tramping to the bottom of the hill. They were at the stage now: a flat clearing in front of the cave, at the bottom of the three hills.

"Why don't you stand here?" Roger directed them to in front of the tree. "I think you'll be able to see better."

"Thank you," signed Dr. Simeon.

Brian pulled away. "I can see fine from here, thanks."

He stood some distance away.

"As you wish," signed Roger.

He strode to the center of the stage area and spread his arms for silence. I peeked down at our audience. They looked as if they'd be pretty tough to please, as if they really didn't want to be there. What if they didn't like us? A shiver went down my spine. What if I forgot everything? What if Nibbles didn't give me the right lines? I'd heard of what I was feeling, but I'd never exactly felt it before and had never thought I would. It's called stage fright.

"Thank you for coming," Roger was signing. "We appreciate your traveling all this distance after a long, hard day to see . . . what we have to show. We've brought you to see a new step forward in primate communications—a step so new and so important, that we can only call it a breakthrough!"

The word went right by me. I sat there frozen, watching the scene.

Roger stole a glance up at me and jerked his head impatiently. "A breakthrough," he repeated as he turned to face his audience. "Truly and certainly a scientific *breakthrough*—"

The word clicked in my mind. "Hoo! Hoo!" I called and stepped out from behind my rock on the ledge above the stage.

Nibbles walked out onto the staging area, just in front of the cave. She looked stiff and nervous—with an even worse case of stage fright than *I* had.

"Nibbles! Nibbles!" I signed. "There are robbers in our house!"

"There are?" She looked up at me.

"They are stealing our home! We must fight them!"

"Fight them," she repeated and stared glassily at the audience.

Dr. Simeon gave a puzzled frown.

"What's going on?" Brian asked. "What are they talking about?"

Roger shrugged. "I'm not sure," he signed. "What are you saying, Danny?" Apparently, this was his idea of improvising.

Brian fidgeted.

Things were not going well. The audience was restless, and Nibbles couldn't even remember her part. She glanced around nervously, apparently confused by the interruption. Amateurs! I'd have to carry it all myself, or there would be no hope at all.

"We must fight them," I signed again.

"Fight them." Nibbles turned—and walked back off stage, straight into the cave! Dr. Simeon squinted, looking even more puzzled than before.

"No, no!" Roger waved frantically to get Nibbles's attention. " 'Where,' " he prompted her.

"Where?" Nibbles stuck her head out.

" 'Where are . . .' " Roger coached.

"Where are . . ." She paused. "Where are they?" she signed, remembering her line at last.

It was the moment I was waiting for. "There!" I pointed at Brian and Dr. Simeon. "The robbers are —*there!*"

It was up to me: my big scene, and my only chance! I caught my breath, grabbed onto the thick vine— and leaped.

"*Aieeeeee!*" I screamed at the top of my lungs. It was as much a sound of fright as a battle cry. "*Aieeeeee!*" I screamed again, as the ledge disappeared behind me.

The wind whistled by me, I was hanging in midair. And suddenly I could take in everything: the blue of the sky, the tree I was swinging toward, the look of sheer surprise and terror on Dr. Simeon's egg-shaped face as I arced toward him. I knew I'd be crashing into him any second, but for a moment everything seemed frozen.

Then I felt a blow to my chest and my whole body, and everything was black for a second. I opened my eyes. I had smacked full-force into Dr. Simeon, slamming him against the tree trunk. It took me a few seconds to clear my head. Then I remembered my part.

"This I do for all chimps everywhere!" I signed with as much conviction as I could muster. I stood up dizzily. "Freedom for chimps!"

Brian was running toward me, his arms outstretched. "You crazy chimp!" he shouted.

It was time to improvise. "Robbers!" I signed and gave another scream. I pounded a tree trunk and jumped up and down. "Trying to rob us of our homes!"

Brian stopped short. I bared my teeth and screamed threateningly. "We've got you now!" I grabbed a branch and charged toward him, dragging the branch behind me. "Dirty robbers!"

The color drained from his face in an instant. He stood frozen—then turned and ran. He raced back up the hill without even looking back.

"That will show you!" I signed. "Freedom for chimps! Freedom for chimps!"

Somewhere inside the cave, someone was screaming and then whimpering, screaming and then whimpering. But I hardly noticed. I felt great. "I did it!" I whooped. "Freedom for chimps!"

Roger walked up and placed some vines in my hand. "Remember your part!" he signed.

I'd nearly forgotten. I turned to Dr. Simeon; he was still dazed, half-sitting against the tree trunk. His safari helmet had rolled away in the dust, and his glasses were bent and stuck at a funny angle. A silly grin covered his face. "Dirty robber!" I signed. I looped a vine around his chest and started tying him to the tree.

"Rrrrrrrgh," said Dr. Simeon and flopped over. I picked him up and started again. It was awkward work, especially with Dr. Simeon so droopy. Once I'd gotten the first vine around him, he kept making feeble movements trying to lift it off and stand up, but I finally got him pretty well secured with about three or four vine ropes.

I sat back and caught my breath, feeling proud and happy. The scene was done. I was still just a little dizzy, but that was nothing to my feeling of accomplishment. I had done it. I had really, really done it. I listened to the sound of my own breathing slowing down to its normal speed, and then noticed the whimpering sound again. I looked. It was Nibbles, walking back and forth, shaking her head. I wondered what was wrong with her.

Dr. Simeon still hadn't said anything, but he looked a little more alert now. "How did you like it?" I signed. He gave me a puzzled look.

"You see, you're supposed to be a robber," I explained. Dr. Simeon's eyes crossed.

I turned to Roger. "We lost half our audience."

Roger nodded. "But they both saw your performance. They must have been very impressed."

Something was wrong: the expression on Roger's face, Nibbles's whimpering, Dr. Simeon's strange reaction. Especially Dr. Simeon. I felt a sinking in my stomach.

"You were really a very *good* robber," I signed to Dr. Simeon. He grinned at me blankly.

I turned to Roger again, trying to recapture the excitement I'd felt just moments before. "I did it!" I signed.

"Yes." Roger smiled faintly. "You certainly did."

≥ 14 ≤
Ambushed!

The sun was nearly set, and Dr. Simeon still hadn't said anything. He just kept looking from side to side and smiling. Nibbles sat on her haunches a little distance away, nibbling nervously at her fingers.

"What now, what now?" she signed.

I was wondering the same thing myself.

"Well, Danny." Roger stroked his chin. "It looks as if you got a little carried away with your part. Most unfortunate."

"Shut up!" I grunted angrily. "You're the one who told me to do it!"

"But I didn't tell you to hit him *that* hard."

The smug jerk! I felt like tearing him apart.

Dr. Simeon's tongue wandered around his mouth and ended up sticking out between his teeth.

Roger eyed him. "I'm afraid the other scientists will take a dim view of this. Makes it rather awkward for all of us."

"What—what will they do to us?" signed Nibbles. Roger didn't answer. "Will they give us a spanking?"

I glanced at Roger. "I guess . . ." I signed slowly. "I guess, maybe now they'll leave us here and never come back."

"If we're lucky," signed Roger.

I looked at him sharply.

"Danny, you don't seem to understand: Attacking a human is a very serious matter—it undermines their authority. They might do . . . *anything.*"

Nibbles covered her eyes. I stared.

Roger placed a hand on my shoulder. I twisted away from him, so mad I could have attacked. Roger put his hand there again, a surprisingly gentle touch, and all of a sudden I was crying, sobbing with my whole body. "I'm sorry! I didn't mean to do it!" I signed. "I didn't mean to hurt him like that, even if he *is* a jerk! I didn't want to get us all in trouble!"

"We know you didn't," Roger signed. For a moment, I thought I saw that glint in his eyes again —a glint that seemed to say he really wanted to burst out laughing—but I couldn't be sure. In an instant the look was gone, if it had ever really been there, and Roger's face was all sympathy.

I controlled myself and looked at Dr. Simeon again. "Do you think he'll be all right?" I asked.

"Hard to say," Roger signed.

"We're in trouble."

Roger nodded. "Tell you what I'll do," he signed at last. "I'll head down to the beach and see if I can put things right with Brian—explain that it was all a mistake, you know."

"Will that be enough?"

Roger shrugged. "It's worth a try."

I swallowed. "I'll come, too."

"No, no, no!" Roger signed quickly. "That's the worst thing you could do. You're the one who Brian saw attack Dr. Simeon, remember? As soon as he sees you coming, he'll either fight or run. If he sees me alone, I might be able to make him listen."

I couldn't argue with that. I nodded.

"You and Nibbles just stay here with Dr. Simeon," Roger continued. "No matter how long it takes, stay put. Understand?"

"All right," I signed.

"And don't forget about the cannibals, either. They're bound to be bolder, now that we're breaking up into smaller groups. If you wander out, they might just pick you off and have chimp stew for supper."

157

Nibbles shuddered.

"Well, just stay close, and you'll probably be okay. Let me see what I can do to get us out of this!"

It was twilight when Roger reached the top of the hill and disappeared along the path toward the beach. I wanted to lie down for a little while, even if actually going to sleep was out of the question. But the ground by the staging area was hard, and Nibbles was afraid to go even a short distance away. So we sat.

So did Dr. Simeon; we avoided looking at him.

"I see a star," signed Nibbles.

"I know."

"My daddy used to show me stars. He told me what their names were."

I sat up. "Stars have names?"

Nibbles nodded gravely. "Yes. Just like people. Every one of them."

"They all look the same to me."

"So do a lot of people."

I nodded.

"We used to look at the stars a lot. Daddy says if you look at the stars you can see shapes in the sky, and he told me all about them."

I squinted up. "What shapes?" They just looked like a bunch of dots to me.

"I don't know," signed Nibbles. "I never really saw the shapes myself. But it was nice when we went out in the back yard and he told me about them."

She paused. "Kathy could see the shapes. I never could, but Kathy knew just what he meant."

"Kathy?"

"His little girl. His *other* little girl."

We were quiet a moment.

"They didn't take *her* away. I'll bet she's with Daddy right now."

She was quiet again.

"I'm scared."

I nodded.

"Do you think we'll ever get back home again?"

"Oh, sure," I signed, though I wasn't sure at all. "Roger will work it out."

She swallowed. "Danny, what did Roger mean, before?"

I looked at her. "When?"

"You know, when he said they might do anything."

"Oh. I don't know. That's just Roger."

"Danny?" She tugged at me. "Will you protect me —if anything happens? Don't let them hurt me."

"Oh . . ." I glanced around uneasily. "I don't think they'll want to hurt you."

"But what if—"

"Just don't worry about it!"

She looked at her hands. "Okay." She was breathing very quickly, so I could tell she was frightened.

"Oh, all right," I signed at last. "I'll make sure nothing happens."

She looked up. "Do you promise?"

"I promise."

"Thank you."

She was quiet again, and I was, too. We sat awhile longer.

We couldn't even hear the waves from down here. I guess the hills blocked out all the sound from the water. There were just the sounds of the island— leaves rustling, an occasional bird call—and then a low moaning, just a little distance away.

We hurried over to Dr. Simeon.

"How are you?" I signed.

Dr. Simeon blinked. "What—" He winced and stopped short, as if just talking in a normal voice hurt him. "My head," he whispered. He was quiet for a moment. "What happened?"

Nibbles and I just looked at him, without answering.

He tried to move his hand and couldn't. He looked down at the vines tying him. "Why. . . ?

"I'll help you," I signed.

I went around the back of the tree and gnawed through the vines, then I came back and faced Dr. Simeon.

Dr. Simeon tried to adjust his glasses, but they were hopelessly bent. He just sat where he was and looked into my eyes for a long time. "Danny," he signed at last. "You attacked me. Why?"

"Well, I didn't really, I—I mean—"

Dr. Simeon shook his head. "You attacked me."

I looked at the ground. "It was supposed to be a play."

He looked at me blankly. For a minute I thought he'd gone under again; then I realized that he was just waiting for me to explain.

"You see, you were supposed to be a robber," I signed, "and we were three chimps. You stole our homes, so we were attacking to get our homes back."

"A play," he repeated. "Like in the theater?"

I nodded.

"You mean, you and the others were actually trying to put on a play? You did it all by yourselves?"

"We thought maybe if we put on a play, maybe you'd take us back home again. And—and maybe then I could be a star."

"Dann—" He spoke it and winced again, even more sharply. "Ugh. . . !" It looked like a nail was being driven into his head every time he spoke.

I couldn't look in his face. I watched my toes.

He tapped me on the shoulder. I had to look up.

"Danny," he signed. "Are you really that unhappy here?"

I nodded.

"Nibbles?"

She nodded, too.

I looked into his eyes.

"Can you take us home now?"

"No." He let out a long breath. "No, I'm sorry, I can't."

"But we're *talking*! We really are!"

"I know." He let out another breath. "But it's not up to me."

"Then who—"

"Some people far, far away, who decide these things. They're very hard to convince."

"They give out the money."

"Dr. Simeon looked at me in surprise. "Yes. They give out the money."

I stood up. "But *we* can make money! If they make me a star, I'll make *lots* of money!"

"Well . . . I'm afraid they have their own ideas about what you should do."

" 'They'?" I stamped my foot. "Who's 'they'? *They* don't know me! How can they decide what I should do?"

"Well, they know a lot *about* you."

"But they don't know *me*!"

"I know. But that's just the way it is." Dr. Simeon looked very tired. "But I'll tell them your suggestion."

I could tell from the way he signed that that wasn't likely to do much good. But it seemed to be all he could do. Nibbles tugged at my hand and looked toward Dr. Simeon. She was right: He didn't look good. I sat down.

"I need help," signed Dr. Simeon. "Where's Brian?"

"He ran away," I signed.

Dr. Simeon grimaced.

"But Roger went to find him and explain everything."

Dr. Simeon leaned his head back. "Danny, next time you do a play, remember: It's just pretend, so be a little more careful, okay?"

I nodded.

"And next time, give a guy a little warning!"

Dr. Simeon closed his eyes, and we all sat quietly for a while.

It was dark now. Just the moon and the stars were lighting the staging area. In the distance I began to hear footsteps and whispered voices. Then the noises stopped, and I heard Roger give a low, calling sound. He repeated it a few more times as he seemed to get closer.

"Hoo! Hoo!" he called from very close now. And there he was, in the clearing at the bottom of the hill, standing in the moonlight.

"Danny!" he signed. "It's okay! Come on out!"

Nibbles and I looked at each other. I stepped out cautiously.

"A little closer, so I can see you! It's safe now, but we have to talk."

I walked a little closer. "Did you find Brian?"

"I can't see what you're signing!" signed Roger, though I could see his signs nearly perfectly. He took a step toward me. "Come on!"

I walked a little closer.

"That's it!" signed Roger. "I've got so much to tell you—"

Suddenly there was a sound like a small explosion, and a whistling sound by my hip. Then another, and another. I stood frozen.

"Danny, that's just—"

Then there was another one, and I was off tearing through the bushes. My heart pounded.

"*Wah! Wah! Wah!*" Roger barked an attack cry.

I turned. Brian and men with guns were rushing into the clearing.

"There he is!" signed Roger and pointed straight at me. "Don't let him get away!"

❧ 15 ❧
Run for My Life!

I didn't stay to watch. I scrambled into the bush and kept going. The men panted and crashed through the underbrush, close behind me.

"There he is! Get him!"

Another shot exploded, then a whole series of them. I raced even harder. I'd never make it this way; somehow I had to lose them. A branch stretched across my path. Without stopping, I swung up on to it, then climbed the tree till I found a protected spot. I stayed very quiet and listened. The explosions stopped.

I hadn't gotten terribly far. I could still hear the voices and pick up a few of the words.

"What the—?"

A voice muttered angrily.

"He's gone."

"I think he went that way. I can still find him."

"Sure you can!"

"Well? Why not?"

"That's jungle! He could be anywhere."

"The chimp says he's dangerous." It was Brian's voice. I peered down toward where the voices were coming from. They were there, standing in the clearing, and Roger was signing to them.

"He says we have to get him," Brian continued, "and he can track him."

Roger nodded vigorously.

I stared. Until now I'd been too frightened to feel anything else. Now I was mad. That animal was trying to kill me! I felt like screaming and jumping right onto him. But I knew that would be foolish.

"Listen, Roger." It was Brian's voice again; I couldn't see his signs too well from where I was, but he was speaking and signing at the same time. "We'll get Dr. Simeon first, if he's still alive. We can always take care of Danny later."

I didn't like the way he said "take care of." It didn't sound like the way it was usually meant.

Roger signed something else.

"*Later*. Remember: unless we get Dr. Simeon

166

back safe and sound, you can just forget about your language lab. You help us, we'll help you; but *only* if we get Dr. Simeon."

So he'd planned it all—right from the start. And I'd fallen into it. I didn't know who I was angrier at —Roger or myself.

"Understand?" asked Brian.

Roger nodded and led them toward the staging area.

I was safe—for the moment.

"What about the other chimp?" asked a voice.

"I wouldn't worry too much about her." It was Brian's voice. "She won't be too hard to handle."

What did he mean? Did he mean that they could get Dr. Simeon back without hurting her? Or that she'd be easy to "take care of" the same way they wanted to "take care of" me? Before tonight I'd never have even thought it of them; now I could believe they'd do anything.

They were walking toward the clearing now— toward Nibbles and Dr. Simeon. There were five all together: Brian and four men carrying guns. The last of the men was passing just under my tree. Just wait here, I was thinking. Just wait here and don't move, and they'll be gone. Gone after Nibbles . . . who had made me make a promise. I snorted. What a dumb thing to have promised her! There was no way I could protect her against men with guns! But still, it was a promise, for whatever that was worth.

And, more, I just didn't like the thought of them hurting her. I had to *do* something; and there was no time to think, no time at all.

Quick, before the last man could pass, I squeezed my eyes shut and for the second time that day I jumped.

"Whupp!" said the man and fell under my weight. I grabbed at his gun.

"Hey!" he shouted. I pulled it out of his hands before he knew what was happening. I had no idea how to use it, but at least that would be one less gun that they could use on *us*. How I'd get the other three guns was a problem I hadn't even thought about.

"Look out!" the man shouted to his friends. "He's got—"

I turned toward him. "Help!" he whimpered in a small voice and hid his head in his hands.

I smiled to myself. He was afraid of me. I jumped up and down once or twice so he wouldn't forget.

"The chimp's got a gun!" shouted one of the other men.

They were running back now, and I heard a shot. I was off in an instant, running through the underbrush.

"We *can't* let him get away *now*!"

Bullets whizzed by me.

I was in the forest now, running deeper into the shadows. The shots and the tramping footsteps were getting farther away, but they weren't stopping. I wondered if taking the gun had been such a good idea.

I could sense where I was, now. I was running uphill—that meant that I was around behind the staging area. Nibbles and Dr. Simeon must be just a short distance below me. Maybe Dr. Simeon could stop the whole thing. They'd *have* to listen to *him*. I ran quietly downhill and crept into the staging area.

"Danny!" Nibbles jumped up and ran to me. "What are they *doing?*"

I didn't answer. I didn't know how; it was just too much to explain. Instead, I just opened my palm and held the gun out to show Dr. Simeon, who was still half-sitting against a tree.

He looked up sharply. "Danny!" He gave the gun a long look. At last he signed. "Do they know you have that?"

I nodded.

Dr. Simeon buried his head in his hands. It seemed forever until he looked up again.

"Danny, Danny . . ." He shook his head. "You have to get rid of that."

"But—"

"Don't argue. You have to throw it away, and they have to *see* you throw it away."

For a moment I couldn't believe it—what he was asking me to do.

"Do it," signed Dr. Simeon. "Do it now." I'd

169

never seen him so determined about anything. "It's the only way."

I had to admit one thing: The gun hadn't seemed to help any. I nodded and crawled a short distance away. Then I knelt and held the gun over my head, above the bushes. "Hoo-hoo," I called, so they'd see me. I waved the gun back and forth, then stood to throw it.

CRACK!

Shots exploded all around me. I dove into the bushes and lay flat on my stomach, but the shots kept coming. The sound alone made me shake. Still the guns fired.

"Stop it! Stop it!" It was Brian's voice. "You can't even see him now; you might hit Dr. Simeon!"

The gunfire stopped.

I lay there for a while, my heart pounding. Suddenly the night was as quiet as if nothing at all had happened. I heard a few whispered voices from where the gunfire had come from, then silence. I caught my breath and crept back to the others.

"Are you all right?" signed Dr. Simeon.

I nodded.

Dr. Simeon let his breath out. His face was white. "I'm sorry," he signed.

Nibbles whimpered.

I sat down heavily.

"You have to talk to them," I signed. "Tell them to stop this!"

"I've been trying!" he signed. "I keep trying!"

Nibbles nodded in agreement.

"Dr. Simeon!" It was Brian's voice again. "Can you hear me? Dr. Simeon!"

Dr. Simeon lifted himself up a little from the trunk he was leaning against. He took a breath and seemed to steel himself.

"Bri—" He winced and stopped short at the sound of his own voice. It wasn't much more than a faint moan.

"Dr. Simeon, are you all right? Can you hear me?"

Dr. Simeon took another breath and tried again, a little louder. "Briii—" His voice cracked, and he winced again. He collapsed back against the tree, panting.

They hadn't heard him.

A tear ran out the corner of Dr. Simeon's eye. "I can't!" he signed. He shook his head gently back and forth. "It's my head. I want to, but I can't!"

I sat watching him. He breathed heavily.

"Dr. Simeon!" Brian called again.

Dr. Simeon started to lift himself again, then gave up.

"Why don't they just come over and talk to us?" I signed to Dr. Simeon. "And let us explain?"

Dr. Simeon looked at me. "Because they know you have a gun, Danny. I think they're afraid that if they come too close, you might shoot them." He paused. "Or me."

171

I shook my head. It was too much, too much. I *had* to get rid of that gun!

I crawled, without rising, to a space between the bushes, then heaved the gun as far as I could into the clearing. Maybe at least they'd hear the sound and come to see what it was. The gun landed with a thud.

"What was that?" called a voice.

"It sounded like it was over that way!"

A man started crawling into the clearing to investigate. He wasn't far from the gun. If he turned just a smidgen, he'd see it; and then there was a rustling sound and Roger scampered out and beat him to it! He made a big show of searching; but meanwhile he'd already found the gun and was quietly kicking it under some vine leaves! Then he picked up a rock and held it high for the men to see.

"It's just a rock!" came the voice again. "He just threw a rock at us."

Roger gave me an evil grin in the moonlight. I growled deep in my throat. For a moment I wanted to end it all right then, to run out into the clearing and at least have the pleasure of throttling Roger with my bare hands before they killed me. Then Roger turned and disappeared into the bushes; I was left there watching, with absolutely nothing I could do.

I crawled back to Nibbles and Dr. Simeon and shook my head. Dr. Simeon seemed weaker now.

"Paper!" he signed, and clutched frantically at his jacket pocket. "I could write them a note, somehow get it to them—" His notepad was not in his pocket; it must have fallen somewhere in the clearing when I first smacked into him that afternoon. There was no way to get it. "Got to stop this!" he signed. Then his eyelids fluttered, and he slumped back against the trunk.

"Dr. Simeon! Dr. Simeon!" Nibbles tugged at his sleeve, but he didn't answer.

His breathing was very light now. He couldn't hear us.

Nibbles and I looked at each other with wide eyes.

A shot sounded from across the clearing.

"Nibbles," I signed, "we've got to get out of here. It's too dangerous."

"What about . . . ?" She glanced at Dr. Simeon.

"We'll put him in the cave. At least then he'll be safe until they figure out that we're gone. Then they can help him."

Nibbles looked doubtful.

"We don't know how to help him, Nibbles. They do."

She looked at Dr. Simeon and nodded.

"We can slip out behind the cave and head up that way." I pointed to the way I'd come down into the staging area.

Nibbles' face filled with terror. "But—but the cannibals . . . !"

"Would you rather stay *here?*"

"The cannibals . . . !" Nibbles repeated.

"Look, which is worse: men with guns, or cannibals we've never even *seen?*" Never even seen. . . . I pounded my fist into my palm. "Nibbles—" I was beginning to see it. "Nibbles—*how do we know that there are cannibals?*"

"Why—the footprints!"

"We know that there are strange footprints. But how do we know that they belong to cannibals?"

"Well, Roger keeps saying—"

"Exactly!" I pounded my fist again. "Because Roger says!"

Come to think of it, Roger seemed to have a "thing" about footprints: first the "cannibal tracks" on the hilltop, then Tarzan's tracks that he'd covered up on the beach. . . . It hit me.

"Nibbles, I'm going to look for those 'cannibals.' "

Her jaw hung open. "Danny—!"

"Don't worry," I cut her off. "I've got a plan. You go in the cave with Dr. Simeon, just in case I'm wrong, and don't come out. I'll be back."

Nibbles started to sign something and then stopped; I guess she could tell that there wasn't any use in arguing with me.

I grabbed one of Dr. Simeon's arms and signaled to Nibbles; she held the other. Then we pulled. I never thought it would be so tough to move him; he'd always seemed so light and skinny. We were panting by the time we got him safely inside the cave. We set him on his back, behind the cave wall, where the guns couldn't get him.

"You stay here," I repeated to Nibbles. "Don't go out, no matter what."

I turned to go.

"Danny . . ." She paused. "Be careful."

I didn't exactly need her to tell me that; but I didn't mind seeing her sign it.

"Okay," I signed.

I crept out the opening and through the underbrush behind the cave. There was open space now. One sound and the men might spot me! I could hear their whispered voices from across the clearing. I stayed close to the ground till I reached more trees. Then I climbed the hill and circled around and down it to the base of the main hill—the one we'd climbed the first day—and the path that we had followed.

The night was still again as I climbed along the path. I heard the broad leaves rustling in the breeze, and a few bird sounds, but no gunfire and no men's voices. The shooting and dangers I'd left just minutes before seemed suddenly unreal, as if they'd never even happened.

In a short time I reached the foliage barrier that we had only once gone beyond. Fighting back my fear, I found the hole we'd cut; it had recently been enlarged—it must have taken days to gnaw a hole that big. So Roger had told the truth about one thing, anyway: They *were* beginning to explore from the other side. I clenched my teeth and slipped through.

I passed the hilltop and began climbing down to the other side of the island. I scanned the path ahead of me in the moonlight, ignoring the marks of birds and small animals, until at last I found what I was looking for: fresh prints like the "cannibal tracks" we'd found our first day on the island. They were footprints slashed by two broad bands that connected each print with the one behind it—tracks that looked to me now very much like a chimp's prints together with tire treads.

My heart beat fast as I followed the tracks. They were close now, I knew it. I rounded a bend, and there they were: Three chimps sitting in a half-circle, each holding the handle of a little red wagon with a computer attached. They stared at me curiously, while continuing to listen for the strange sounds from the other side of the island that had probably awakened them some time before.

A fourth computer wagon stood a short distance away, under a tree.

We stared at each other for a few moments; nobody moved. Then a small throat-clearing sound from over my head broke the silence. I jumped.

There, in the tree above me, sat Tarzan, looking down at me intently.

⚘ 16 ⚘
Tarzan

I gave a weak grunt of greeting. "Hi, Tarzan," I signed. "Good to see you!"

Tarzan just stared.

I grinned nervously. "Oh. Well, I know you don't know sign language, but this just means 'hi,' that's all." I gave the greeting grunt again.

Tarzan smiled faintly and jumped to the ground. He turned to his friends and mimicked my sign, then flipped on his computer and punched a few keys. His friends crowded around to see the symbols on the screen—and burst out laughing. Tarzan laughed too and again mimicked me.

Anger flashed through me. I grunted and stamped my feet.

"Listen, you—!" I signed.

Tarzan raised his eyebrows innocently; he shrugged his shoulders and shook his head. Then he pointed to his machine.

I got the message. Tarzan was telling me I'd have to talk to him in his own language.

"Listen—" I signed again.

Tarzan shook his head and led me by the hand around to the front of the computer. He pointed to the keyboard.

I stared at it hopelessly. The symbols meant absolutely nothing to me.

Tarzan punched two keys to produce a symbol on the screen. His friends hooted. Then he turned to me and made a single sign. My jaw hung open: Tarzan was calling me an *insect*!

The nerve of him! I growled and bared my teeth —and then stopped myself. *Insect* was the one word we had taught Tarzan in all the time he had lived on our side of the island. He was just giving me back some of my own treatment.

I took a breath. "Tarzan, I know we were kind of tough on you before," I signed, "and I just want to say I'm sorry . . ."

Of course he didn't understand me. He shook his head and turned away.

This could go on forever! Meanwhile Nibbles and Dr. Simeon could be getting shot to death; and only Tarzan could help.

I walked after him and grabbed his elbow. "Come!" I signed.

He shook me off.

I gave the danger call and grabbed his elbow again, more insistently. He again broke free, angrily this time, and his friends formed a threatening circle around me. I backed off; they let me slip through their circle and stood there as a barrier between me and Tarzan.

Tarzan picked up the handle of his computer wagon and turned to leave.

"Hoo-hoo!" I called for his attention.

He gave me a look that seemed to say, "Well?"

Somehow I *had* to communicate with him. With my fingers I formed circles around my eyes to indicate Dr. Simeon's glasses. Then I pulled myself up to my full height and held my hand as high as I could reach it, to show a very tall person. With my face I imitated Dr. Simeon's "Hi-Gang-Isn't-Everything-Great!" expression. Then I mimed putting on Dr. Simeon's safari hat.

Tarzan cocked his head; at least he was watching.

Now I pretended to fall and bang my head, then to try to get up; then I lay flat on my back, with my eyes closed.

I opened my eyes.

Tarzan wrinkled his brow and signaled for his friends to be still. I repeated my performance.

Tarzan gave me a hard look. I guessed he might be wondering if I was telling the truth or was just trying another trick. I looked him full in the face.

Tarzan grunted. He punched some keys on his computer. His friends read the message and looked at him sharply. Then they punched back their own messages; Tarzan punched back one more message, and his friends cleared the path for him.

Something still bothered me: Tarzan deserved to have some idea of what he was getting into. I gave the danger call again and pointed to the other side of the island, hoping he'd understand me. Tarzan studied me a long moment; then he picked up the handle of his wagon and grunted to me; I nodded and led the way.

It was almost dawn when we reached the hill behind the cave. Everything seemed quiet beyond the clearing; but I knew that Brian and the other men must still be watching. We had to work fast now. Once the men could see, they might not be so worried about hitting Dr. Simeon by mistake; they might rush in shooting before we had a chance to explain. So we had to do it before daylight. I hoped with all my might that Dr. Simeon was awake now; if he couldn't help us, we'd never make it.

We were almost at the cave, but we had to break from the path to get down there. I hadn't thought about that. It was one thing for one lone chimp to slip through the underbrush undetected; it was very different for two chimps with a heavy computer wagon. I stood there thinking a moment; then I grabbed some leafy branches and piled them over the wagon to make it harder to spot. We could never wheel it down, that much was obvious. I lifted one end of it.

Tarzan looked at me in alarm and grabbed to protect his wagon. I just jerked my head in the direction of the cave. Tarzan followed with his eyes and hesitated; then he picked up the other end of the wagon. I signaled him to be quiet. As carefully as we could, we carried it down the hill.

We were more than halfway down—so far no problems. I could see us back in the cave again, safe and sound. . . . Thump! I tripped and went crashing through the bushes. Somehow we landed the wagon right-side-up, but the sound . . . !

A strong light flashed on from the clearing. It scanned the hillside, back and forth, back and forth. We froze where we were; my heart pounded. I don't know how close that light came to us, because my eyes were shut tight most of the time. But it must have been pretty close, because I could see red through my eyelids.

It seemed forever until the light turned off, and

then even longer before we dared move again. Tarzan gave me a long, scared look. He must have wondered what I had dragged him into.

At last we picked up the wagon again and carried it down toward the cave. I could see a little bit of light starting across the sky, but it was still dark beneath the hills in the staging area. We set the wagon down carefully and rolled it the last short distance into the cave.

"Danny!" Nibbles ran at me and gave me a hug; I hugged back, as hard as I could. "Glad, glad!"

"Thanks!" I signed. "I'm glad, too."

She nodded.

"I've brought Tarzan back to help us."

Tarzan hung back toward the cave opening.

"Thank you," signed Nibbles to Tarzan.

Tarzan lowered his eyes.

Dr. Simeon was lying on the ground, facing the cave wall. He *had* to help us now! I knelt by him and tugged at his hand.

"Dr. Simeon. Dr. Simeon!"

He didn't answer.

"Dr. Simeon! Dr. Simeon!" I tugged again. "Dr. Simeon!"

Dr. Simeon opened an eye.

"Dr. Simeon! I brought back Tarzan and his machine!"

He lifted his head. "What?"

"We've got Tarzan's machine! Now you can type them a message and explain everything!"

He sat up and took in the scene. It took him a moment to understand. Then his face broke out into a tremendous grin. "Danny, you figured out a way! And Tarzan!" I thought I saw a tear in the corner of his eye.

Tarzan wheeled over his machine, and Dr. Simeon started typing. I could guess what he was saying: He was explaining the situation to Tarzan and asking to borrow his machine.

Tarzan's mouth opened, and his eyes got wide. I could imagine what he felt like. After all he'd gone through to get that machine, his only way of speaking and understanding, and now . . .

Dr. Simeon typed some more. Tarzan hesitated. Then he typed a short message. Dr. Simeon read it and put an arm around Tarzan. Tarzan just stood there looking down, pressing his lips together as tight as they'd go. I thought any minute he'd burst out crying. Then he turned and walked deeper into the cave and stood with his back to us. I wished there were something I could say to him, but I didn't know how. He seemed to want to be alone. And now there was no time.

"Dr. Simeon," I signed. "Tell them we won't hurt you. Tell them we won't hurt them or anybody, if they just won't shoot!"

Dr. Simeon nodded and typed a series of the strange symbols. "This should do it," he signed.

Nibbles and I wheeled the wagon out toward the cave opening. Tarzan didn't help us move it; he just stayed in the corner with his back to us.

Nibbles and I gave a push, and the wagon rolled out into the staging area. The TV screen glowed its message in the darkness toward the men's position across the clearing.

For a moment everything was still. Then there was a shot. One of the front wheels gave a jump. The wagon jerked and came down at a funny tilt. Tarzan winced and covered his eyes. He almost looked as if he'd been shot himself. Then there was another shot and another.

The idiots! Couldn't they *see?* Did the wagon *look* like a chimp?!

Another shot.

So we'd failed. It was almost light now. Any minute they'd be upon us, before they even recognized the message. And then it would all be over.

More shots.

Can't you LOOK?! I wished I could scream it at them. *Can't you even LOOK?!*

Someone was looking, and didn't like what he saw. With a screech, Roger came rushing out from the bushes, swinging a big stick over his head, aiming straight for the computer!

Then everything seemed to happen at once. Without warning, Roger swerved in his path, bringing the stick around to hit the computer from the side. Just as he swerved, another shot rang out. Roger's face went blank; he spun around and thudded to the earth, trailing a little spray of red in the air behind him. Something in the bushes stirred. In an instant, men were rushing out, charging toward us, crouched to the ground, firing as they ran.

"Get 'em!" cried one. "Into the cave!"

Bullets tore into the ground before the cave opening. Rocks jumped with the gunfire; the sound was deafening. I flattened myself to the floor, my heart pounding.

They were almost to the cave now. I could see their guns pointing toward us . . .

"*Stop it! Hold your fire!*"

It was Brian's voice.

"What the—" The man closest to us dove to the ground, then looked back toward Brian. "Get down, you fool!" He lifted his gun again and shot.

"*Stop it!*" Brian was standing behind a bush across the clearing; he held a pair of binoculars to his eyes and stared through them at the TV screen. "*Stop it, I said!*"

The other gunmen hit the ground.

"*STOP SHOOTING!*"

The air was suddenly quiet; the gunfire stopped.

I looked first to Nibbles, then to Dr. Simeon, and finally back in the far corner to Tarzan. We looked at each other silently, then I turned and looked out again toward Brian.

Brian let the binoculars drop from his hand. "It's a message," he said in a quiet voice. "A message from Dr. Simeon!"

❧ 17 ❧
Aftermath

We walked out with our hands up and were blinded by bright lights suddenly glaring at us in the early morning twilight. I squinted and tried to see. Then the lights wents off for a few moments. Between the black spots the lights had left in front of my eyes, I could dimly make out the shapes of cameras and microphones.

Then the men went into the cave with two poles wrapped in canvas. When they came out, Dr. Simeon was lying on his back on the canvas, and the men were carrying him between the two poles; I think someone called it a stretcher.

Dr. Simeon was signing something to Brian. I guess his head still hurt too much for him to speak. Then the people with the cameras and microphones were running over to him and asking him questions, but Brian made them stop.

Meanwhile, one of the men was kneeling over Roger. Roger was raising his head, and the man was tying strips of cloth around Roger's shoulder. The strips got stained dark red as soon as the man tied them on. Another man took off his shirt and found some branches, and they made another stretcher for Roger.

Tarzan rushed over to his computer wagon and started anxiously punching keys, apparently checking the machine for damage. The computer itself seemed unharmed, but the wagon wheels were locked. He pulled and he dragged, frantically trying to move the machine, but it hardly budged. He shot a pained, accusing glance at Dr. Simeon. I ran over and lifted one end; and together, we half-dragged, half-carried the wagon.

They marched us back to the beach that way, Tarzan and I carrying his computer wagon, Roger and Dr. Simeon on stretchers, Nibbles and Brian walking ahead of us, and the film crew trooping behind us. The film crew was constantly buzzing, but none of the rest of us said or signed much.

I dropped back a bit with Tarzan to walk next to

Roger. He was resting calmly on his stretcher, from time to time looking out to observe the ride.

I looked down at him. You'd think he might at least be a little embarrassed and turn away or something. But he just kept looking up at me, right in the eyes, as if he had nothing in the world to be ashamed of. I could feel my face getting warm with anger.

"You tried to kill us!" I signed. "Just so you could get your lousy language lab!"

Roger looked at me mildly. "I offered you a chance, Danny," he signed with his uninjured arm. "You and Nibbles could have been respected colleagues in my lab. But you turned me down. What other choice did I have then—either rot away on this island or perhaps go back to being a lab specimen myself? I did what I had to do."

"You mean you tried to kill us."

"Danny, Danny." Roger shook his head. "And what of *your* plan? Correct me if I'm wrong, but didn't that call for you to run off to Hollywood and become a star—while leaving Nibbles and me to the cannibals? Was that idea so much nobler than mine?"

I didn't sign anything. It wasn't as bad as what Roger had done, but it wasn't exactly something to be proud of, either.

"You did what you had to," Roger continued,

"just as I did. Only I was smarter about it, so I deserve to succeed. Survival of the fittest."

"You don't look so fit right *now*."

Roger smiled ruefully. "Yes, a slight miscalculation. I'm afraid I got a little carried away." Roger closed his eyes. "But don't worry about me, Danny."

"What's that supposed to mean?"

"Public relations," Roger signed. "Public relations."

I had no idea what that meant. But Roger wasn't watching, and I had nothing more to say to him. One of the men shouted an order, and Tarzan and I dropped back into line.

At the beach, the film crew set up again. A young woman stood in front of the camera and started talking into a microphone, while a man stood two steps behind her and translated into sign language.

"This is Tracy Evans, Channel Three News," said the woman, "and with me I have Mark Thomas, whom some of you may recognize as the little man in the corner of the screen on our eleven-thirty nightly rebroadcast for the hearing impaired.

"It's been an exciting ending to a very tense night, here on Chimp Island. For any of you who may have missed it, let me repeat our earlier report: Dr. Simeon *has* been safely recovered, and the rebel chimps *are* now in custody.

"Together with Mark, I'm now going to attempt an exclusive Channel Three interview with the chimp called Roger, the hero of this hostage situation."

Roger looked more alert now; he was sitting up a short distance from Mark.

"As you know," the woman continued, "it was Roger who relayed the rebel chimps' threats and demands to research assistant Brian Girard and led Mr. Girard and the rescue team to the rebel hideout. He then spoke in sign language with Dr. Simeon's captors and finally was wounded only minutes before the crisis ended, when he bravely ran into the field to draw Mr. Girard's attention to the message from Dr. Simeon."

The woman turned to Roger. "First, Roger, on behalf of all our viewers, I'd like to express our appreciation for all you've done tonight. To see such bravery and selflessness in a chimp is truly remarkable."

"Thank you, Tracy," signed Roger.

Mark repeated the words aloud.

"Roger," the woman continued, "what made you do it?"

"Well, Tracy, I've always been a strong believer in understanding between the species, and when I saw what these other chimps were doing, well, it was just destroying the basis of understanding and communication that we'd all worked so hard to build up. I couldn't let that happen. And I certainly couldn't let a great language researcher like Dr. Simeon be lost."

"I see," said Tracy.

"After all," Roger continued, "if we want humans to treat us with the respect and dignity we deserve, then we have to show the same to humans. And when you come right down to it, isn't that what communication is really all about?"

"Well, I think there's a lesson in that for all of us," said Tracy.

"As a matter of fact—" Roger half-smiled. It looked to me as he was trying—and failing—not to look *too* pleased with himself. "As a matter of fact, Tracy, when all this is over, I would like nothing better than to simply continue my studies. Perhaps scientists could fund a modest little language lab somewhere where I could pass on to other chimps some of what I've learned myself: an institute for interspecies understanding. Just a dream, perhaps, but one that I think we'll see as a reality."

"Well, Roger—" Tracy's face brightened. "I think we may have a more exciting way than that of achieving your goal."

"Yes?"

"I've been in radio contact with one of our producers in Hollywood. He's been watching you all night, and he's very impressed. As a matter of fact, he tells me that he's made some very *big plans* for you!"

The smile faded from Roger's face. "Big plans?"

"Our network is planning a new comedy series: all about a chimp who works as a bellboy at a luxury hotel! And Mr. Carlton has authorized me to tell you that they want *you* for the part!"

"Oh—" Roger sat up straight. "Oh, well, I—I'm very flattered of *course*, but I couldn't *possibly*—!"

"Oh, don't be so modest, Roger!" said Tracy. "We think you'd be wonderful for the part. And just think, with millions of people watching you every week—talk about understanding between the species! And you'd get to wear a little red suit."

"A *suit?*" Roger signed weakly.

"And a little red hat!"

"A *hat?*" Roger gulped. "No, no, no, this is impossible! If you want an actor, you should see my friend Danny. Now *there's* an actor! Danny— Danny!" Roger scanned the beach, looking for me. "Just let him show you what he can do! Danny!"

If ever I had a chance, this was it.

But last night, I had had to run for my life. Men had tried to shoot me down, without even a second thought or a chance to explain. Somehow, this morning, the idea of being a clown for a bunch of humans just didn't seem so appealing anymore.

I slipped into the bushes.

"Danny! Danny!" Roger signed frantically. "Please come out—*please!* It's your big chance!"

"Roger—" said Tracy, "we know you're modest, but really—"

"Danny!" He turned to Tracy. "Please understand —this is impossible, really it is. Brian *promised*—!"

Two of the rescue team rushed over. "I think he's getting overexcited," said one.

"Yes," Tracy said to Roger. "You relax, and we'll talk more at a better time."

"Danny!" signed Roger. The men lifted the stretcher. "Danny! Come out!"

There was panic in his eyes as they carried him away.

✹ 18 ✹
Home

I kept wishing that somehow Roger would have more of a punishment—something to really make him pay for all he had done to us. I imagined things like putting him in jail for life, or locking him in language lab every moment he was awake, and worse. But then I remembered how he'd kept us going, how he'd *made* us survive while we were on our own— whatever his real reasons had been. I had to admit it: Roger had kept us alive. It didn't make up for what he'd tried to do later, but at least it helped me stop thinking about it. Anyway, he was off the island now.

And maybe, for a chimp as proud as Roger, the TV series would be almost bad enough.

A short time after the interview, all the humans had left the island. They loaded Dr. Simeon into a helicopter, and Roger along with him; the rest left in two motor boats. I don't know what they were originally planning to do with us, but Dr. Simeon had a long talk in sign language with Brian, and they finally decided to do nothing, at least for the time being. Brian looked in on us every few days; but he didn't trust us and we didn't trust him, so we didn't have much to say to each other.

I helped Tarzan carry his wagon back to his friends on the other side of the island. I felt bad that now he could never move very far from one spot and still be able to talk. But there was nothing else I could do to help.

Life seemed to settle into a routine; food gathering, eating, sleeping. But I didn't let myself get too comfortable. I had the feeling that, far away, people were making decisions about us. We waited.

Then one morning Nibbles and I heard the motorboat puttering up to the beach. Even at a distance, we saw that there were two people in it. They were Brian and Dr. Simeon.

Dr. Simeon had a bandage on his head, under his safari hat, and he looked a little pale, but otherwise he seemed okay.

"Hello!" he said and signed as he got out of the boat.

Nibbles and I ran to him.

"How are you?" I asked.

"Okay," he signed. "Better." He seemed a little quieter than before, and his grin wasn't quite as animated. But that was okay; it didn't seem so fake this time. Nibbles and I each took one of his hands, and he didn't say anything for a long time; I think he liked that.

"What's that?" I signed, pointing to something glinting inside the boat.

"Oh." Dr. Simeon smiled. He walked to the boat and pulled away the plastic wrapping so we could see. Inside was a wagon, a brand new one, with racing stripes and sparkles.

"It's for Tarzan," he signed.

I was glad. Now Tarzan could move around with his computer again. And he'd have the nicest wagon on the whole island.

"So . . ." Dr. Simeon sat down on the beach, and we sat in front of him. Brian stayed back by the boat.

"So . . ." said Dr. Simeon. "Remember those people I told you about?" he signed. "The people far away who decide things?"

I nodded. I knew something was coming; my heart thumped, and my breaths came short.

"I've been talking with them. They said that this

197

time they'll listen to what you want before they decide."

I swallowed. "Does that mean they'll send me wherever I want?"

"No," Dr. Simeon signed, "it doesn't. But it means they'd at least like to know what you really want before they decide."

I waited.

"I told the scientists all about everything that happened here: The way you sign to me and to each other, your play, how you communicated with the chimps on the other side of the island. The scientists were impressed. What they think they would really like . . ." Dr. Simeon paused uncomfortably. "What they'd really like is to study you here, to see what kind of a community you develop, how you live together and cooperate, just watch and see what you can do for yourselves on your own, now that you have language."

"That's what they'd really like," I signed.

"There is one other possibility." He paused again. "I guess you know that Roger is doing a TV series."

"The scientists let him go?"

"They're kind of afraid of him. You see, *we* all know what he *really* did; but to the public he's a hero. They're not about to give him his own language lab *now*. But it wouldn't look right for them to seem ungrateful, either. So they're letting the network have him. They felt it was either that, or tell the world how Roger fooled us." He smiled sheepishly. "And that wouldn't have made us scientists look very bright."

I saw his point.

Dr. Simeon looked at me. "There's room for one more chimp on the series—a sort of sidekick to Roger. When I heard about that, of course I thought of you. They say Roger put in a good word for you, too—said you could even have *his* part if they'd let him go; but, of course, that's out of the question."

"Roger's sidekick."

"Yes."

Working with Roger and with humans. Roger I *knew* was a sneak. And humans—they'd never *really* respect us, even if I was a star. Of all the humans I'd known in my whole life, there had only been two I could really trust, who'd really treated me like a person—and one of them was Dr. Simeon, of all people. The other had been Peggy, way back in Dr. Franklin's lab.

I could still be a star. They were giving me one more chance, probably the last one I'd ever get. I took a deep breath.

"I think I'd rather stay here, on the island, with other chimps."

"You're sure of that?"

I nodded.

"I think that's a good decision." Dr. Simeon paused one more time. "Nibbles," he began. "Nibbles . . ."

"I've been thinking a lot," Nibbles broke in. "I love my daddy. But I like being with Danny, too, and Daddy never even came to see me. Even when they were *shooting* at me!" She looked down at her hands; for a minute I thought she was about to cry. "But *Danny* came back, just like he promised. He didn't let them hurt me." She looked at me shyly, out of the corner of her eye. "I don't want Danny to be here all alone. I'll stay here with Danny." She looked back at Dr. Simeon. "You explain to Daddy for me."

I had one last dream that night, the night Dr. Simeon left. The big female chimp was carrying me again, through the same jungle I'd seen before. I saw the leaves, the fruits, the greens, the yellows. But I felt a little older now, and I wasn't hanging from her chest anymore; now I was right side up, riding on her back. I looked out at the scenery, over the back of her head, and tried again to see her face. Then she stopped, and I jumped down; as I did, I seemed to catch just a glimpse of gentle eyes. In an instant I had hooted and scampered away, excited to be exploring the trees and the leaves around me. When I looked back she was gone—and I knew that she was gone for good. But I wasn't frightened; I felt I knew where I was. And I also felt that somewhere the big chimp was still watching me—and that she liked what she saw.

We've been here two years now—I know because that's what Dr. Simeon tells me. He comes by two or three times a year to take notes. When he comes we talk, and we share some oranges and bananas (he lets *us* keep all the leaves and termites), and we walk around the island. He also brings fresh batteries for the computers.

Dr. Simeon let it slip once that Nibbles's daddy is working with a dolphin now. Apparently there's lots of money for scientists to work with dolphins, and Nibbles's daddy was probably studying up on it before they even sent us to Chimp Island. We decided it would be best not to tell Nibbles about it.

We visit Tarzan and the computer chimps on the other side of the island every once in a while. We've learned how to type a few things on their computers, and they've learned a few signs, but we haven't gotten terribly far, and sometimes I don't know what in the world they're talking about. But at least no one calls anyone an insect.

Nibbles and I never did get to like the shed the humans built for us. Dr. Simeon showed us how our parents used to sleep in trees, bending leafy branches over to make nests, so we tried that for a few nights; but somehow, after having lived in houses, that didn't feel right, either. So we moved into the cave.

That has worked out fine, and it's a nice part of the island to live in. Nibbles decided to decorate, to make the place a little less dingy. So she mixed up some berries and water and different kinds of mud to make some paints and started rubbing them over the cave walls. I was surprised, because I'd never seen her figure anything out or invent anything for herself before. But she said she wanted to make it look like home. At first she only painted big, broad areas in one color, as if she were painting a wall in a house. But then she started making little drawings, too; humans and houses and cars and bicycles. I asked her what she was doing, and she said that that was for our kids, so that one day they'd know what civilization was like.

Well, I wasn't so hot on that idea—having little chimps, I mean. The computer chimps on the other side of the island have one already (which is probably what gave her the idea), and he seems like more trouble than he's worth. But Nibbles just smiled and signed, "We'll see," and kept on painting.

And, I have to admit, some of the pictures are really nice.

My favorite is one I think I'm not supposed to know about. It's far away from the ones she did for the kids, way around a corner in the back part of the cave, where a little light shines onto it from a crack at sunset. She spent a long time working on it when she thought I wasn't watching. She usually looks at it for a little while before she goes to sleep each evening. The picture makes me think a little bit about Peggy. I don't know exactly why it should, because it's obviously Nibbles's family, not mine, but it does; and once in a while I look at it, too.

The picture shows a man and a woman and a little girl and a chimp and a cat, all standing together and looking at the stars.